RUNNING OUT OF TIME

Running out of Time

Gareth Evans

translated from the Welsh by Jane Burnard

Gwasg Carreg Gwalch

First published in Welsh as *Gethin Nyth Brân*, 2017
Published in English: 2022

ISBN: 978-1-84527-896-0

Ebook ISBN: 978-1-84524-511-5

Published with the financial support of the Books Council of Wales

Cover design: Anne Cakebread

Published by Gwasg Carreg Gwalch,
12 Iard yr Orsaf, Llanrwst, Wales LL26 0EH
tel: 01492 642031
email: books@carreg-gwalch.cymru
website: www.carreg-gwalch.cymru

Published and printed in Wales

To the children, Ioan and Manon,

who aren't children any more.

PART 1

1

There was no escape. Gethin battled his way up the slope through the thick, black forest. With every step he took the bloodthirsty beast closed in on him. It was too dark to see much, but between the branches Gethin made out flashes of colour under the cold light of the moon: green, staring eyes, sharp, yellow teeth, bared in a snarl, and a long tail that slid like a snake through the leaves. Gethin tried to run faster, but the ground was like sticky treacle and instead of speeding up he was slowing down. Behind him he heard a deafening roar – the creature was at his nape. The next moment Gethin fell, outstretched on the ground, and the monster's maw was gaping wide over him. He closed his eyes tightly as the beast's saliva dripped down to soak his face. Then came the pain – beyond anything Gethin had ever suffered – as its claws pierced his chest, penetrating his ribcage and tearing it open.

~

Gethin awoke, dripping with sweat. He wasn't in a dark forest after all, but his own bed. Relief swept over him as he realised that the whole thing had been a nightmare. But the relief didn't last long. Because the pain in his chest was still there and real life was a bit like a nightmare at the moment anyway.

He listened to his chest rattling, exactly like his grandfather's did when the weather turned. Rolling over to try to ease the pain, he stared at the numbers on the digital alarm clock that shone through the early-morning greyness. Five minutes to seven. Five minutes before the alarm went. There was no point going back to sleep.

Gethin got up, shivering, though it wasn't very cold. He switched off the alarm and put the light on. His chest still hurt. He tried to control his breathing – his mam would come into the room any minute now to make sure he was up, and he didn't want her knowing anything was wrong.

In a moment of panic – he had jitters like this sometimes – he stared about him to make sure everything was still in its proper place: the globe atlas that lit up, his books, the rectangular glass case that was home to his pet, and the poster of Mo Farah on the wall. Order was important, especially in his own bedroom – the only place Gethin felt completely safe.

As he dressed, he heard his mam's voice seeping through the house. But she wasn't calling Gethin. Soon he realised that another voice was competing with hers. A man's voice. His mam and his tad-cu – his grandfather – were at each other's throats, as usual. Gethin closed his eyes tightly and pressed his hands against his ears.

Suddenly, everything went quiet. And then a door slammed shut. Gethin sat on the edge of his bed, waiting for his mam to call him. He waited. And waited. And waited some more. Not a peep of sound now. He began to feel uneasy. At last, he plucked up enough courage to go downstairs.

Gethin crept past the middle room, which had been his tad-cu's bedroom ever since he'd become unable to manage the stairs. Then he entered the kitchen and saw his mam standing there, stock still, staring out of the window. She didn't notice him. She was far, far away. Silence filled the room, like rank, freezing fog. Gethin stood, motionless, waiting for her to come back to herself.

Her name was Helen. When she smiled, her face lit up and she'd look really young. But she didn't smile often. She worked in a call centre, answering stupid questions all day. And on top of that, she had to look after her dad – or Gransha, as his tad-cu insisted Gethin call him. After Gransha's condition had worsened, about three months ago, Gethin and his mam had moved into his house on the outskirts of Pontypridd.

Without warning, Gethin's mam turned from the window and faced him.

"What are these?" she demanded, thrusting the palm of her hand towards him. Gethin stared in surprise. Cigarette butts.

"They were in your bag," said his mam.

Gethin knew at once who'd done it. Cai Thomas.

"I didn't put them there," he said quickly, telling the truth.

"I should hope not. But who did?"

He didn't dare tell her his suspicions. Didn't dare tell her about Cai, who was forever tormenting him. Nor about everyone else at his new school, who either mocked him or ignored him. Not, if Gethin was completely honest, that things had been much better in his old school.

"Just the boys, having a laugh."

"I for one don't think it's very funny."

Gethin squirmed as his mam searched his face for a sign that he wasn't telling the truth. He felt his breathing getting faster, and was afraid his chest would start wheezing again.

"Everything's all right at school, is it?"

"Yes, course it is," answered Gethin, a little too quickly.

"Because if you're being bullied, you need to tell me."

"I know, Mam. But everything's fine, honest."

His mam looked at him again, sharply. Did she believe him?

"OK. But can you please tell your friends not to do something so stupid again," she ordered.

Gethin nodded. He didn't want any more questions. He must've looked convincing because his mam went upstairs to finish dressing, complaining that, thanks to Gethin, she'd be late for work.

He didn't want breakfast at all by now, so he stuffed a handful of cornflakes into his mouth and munched away without bothering with a bowl, never mind milk. He thought about the day ahead at school, and his heart sank.

He'd dropped a few cornflakes on the table. Collecting them carefully he put them into his mouth and, as he crunched on them, Gethin realised just how lonely he was.

2

The school bus was late. Other schoolkids were huddled under the plastic roof of the bus shelter, but Gethin preferred to stand apart, despite the fact that he was surrounded by a big cloud of drizzling rain, whose drops pricked his skin like tiny insects. He didn't care about being soaked. Because the bus was late, there'd be less time standing about in the schoolyard before registration – and that was a good thing. Gethin hated the noise of the yard before the first bell: the shouting, the laughing and the screaming.

He saw the bus approach, creeping through the rain. It halted a little before the bus stop, the brakes hissing as wheels splashed water everywhere. Kids rushed to get on to the bus and out of the rain, and some of the girls were screeching and giggling. Gethin was the last on. Finding an empty seat he sat down quickly, leaning his forehead against the cold, damp window. He could hardly see outside. It was as if the world had disappeared.

He heard the angry hissing of the bus again, as the vehicle prepared to join the traffic. Then a crunch as it changed gear, and a roar as it speeded up. Like the roar of the beast in the nightmare. Gethin shivered as he remembered. It hadn't been his first nightmare, but it'd been the first where he'd come face to face with such a terrifying creature.

"Aw!!!"

Someone cried out in pain, making Gethin jump in his seat. Turning, he witnessed Cai Thomas rubbing the top of a red-haired boy's head with his fist, back and forth, hard, as if he was trying to scrub it clean. Gethin had noticed the boy before, and his two friends, who were sitting behind him. The three of them were always together, wandering the edge of the yard, doing their best to keep away from everyone and everything. Gethin had coined a name for them: 'Y Tri Trist' – or 'The Sad Three'.

"Oi! What you looking at?" spat Cai, in his direction. Cai was the only boy in his year who was shorter than Gethin, but he had a bigger mouth than anyone, a mouth that picked on Gethin every day. As if that wasn't bad enough, Cai was Nathan Jenkins's lapdog – and Nathan Jenkins was the hardest boy in the year. So no one dared cross Cai. Not that Gethin was brave enough to do so, in any case.

The relief on the red-haired boy's face was obvious as Cai let go of him and turned his attention to Gethin.

"Did Mami give you a row about the cigarettes? Baaad boy."

"No . . ." protested Gethin.

"That's a shame," said Cai, clenching his fist, preparing to hurt him. By now Nathan was also staring in Gethin's direction – through sleepy eyes, as if the whole thing bored him. But Gethin know very well that Nathan was taking it all in.

The next moment Gethin jolted forward as the bus braked suddenly. He saw Cai stagger and grab at one of the seats to stop himself falling on his backside. Some of the older kids laughed at him, and Cai frowned.

When he'd recovered, Cai marched down the aisle towards Gethin. But one of the girls who'd just got on the bus was standing in his way, blocking him. Gethin stared at her in surprise, but he wasn't half as surprised as Cai.

"That's my seat," Cai protested, pointing at the empty seat next to Gethin.

"It's my seat now," answered the girl defiantly, sitting down quickly. As the other girls took up the empty seats around her she turned to Cai, who was still glaring at them all.

"You deaf, or what?" she asked him.

Cai turned on his heel, swearing under his breath.

"You OK?" the girl asked Gethin.

"Yes, thanks," answered Gethin, shyly.

She gave him a smile before turning to her friends. As they chattered and laughed, putting on more make-up and comparing messages on their expensive phones, Gethin turned to look out the window. He felt his cheeks blush – another thing that annoyed him about himself – and he didn't want the girls to notice, especially the girl who was sitting next to him.

Her name was Caitlin Derbyshire. Her hair was black as a raven's wing and her eyes were almost as dark – eyes that sparkled when she laughed. And she laughed a lot. She, without doubt, was the star of the class, and all the other girls were dying to be her friend.

Gethin had noticed her on his first day at this new school, but he'd never plucked up enough courage to say a word to her.

"Oh, that's so cute!" said Caitlin, aiming her mobile phone at the window. Without realising it, Gethin had drawn a smiley face with his finger on the steamed-up window. Caitlin snapped a picture of it with her phone. Some of the other girls did the same.

"I'm going to put it on Instagram," said Caitlin. "You can like it, if you want."

"I'm not on Instagram," said Gethin.

It was Caitlin's turn to look surprised. She stared at him, incredulous. "I couldn't LIVE without Instagram," she announced. The other girls agreed with her, enthusiastically.

Gethin felt himself blushing again. Then he heard a familiar voice, mocking him from the back of the bus.

"Loser!" shouted Cai.

"Only one loser on this bus – and that's you, Cai Thomas," shouted back Caitlin, her dark eyes flashing.

Gethin could have sworn he saw Cai, of all people, blush. And even more unexpectedly, he made out a playful little grin on Nathan's face.

"Never mind. I'll send you the picture. What's your number?" Caitlin asked Gethin.

Gethin gave her his number and within a blink the image was on his phone. He looked at the little round face, smiling up at him. And, for once, there was a wide smile on Gethin's face, too.

3

"Any idea what 'Pontypridd' means?"

Mr Davies Cymraeg – the Welsh teacher – was asking, but no one was answering. Gethin was very fond of Mr Davies. He was always in a good mood, and he always looked fit and well because he liked walking in the Welsh mountains in his spare time, making a note of any interesting place names he came across on the way.

"What if I told you that it used to be 'Pont-y-tŷ-pridd'?" suggested Mr Davies.

Silence, again. Gethin thought he knew the answer. Pont meant bridge. Tŷ meant house. And pridd meant earth or soil. But he wasn't about to volunteer until he saw Caitlin smiling at him, encouragingly. Then, to his own surprise, he put up his hand.

"Yes, Gethin?" Mr Davies was obviously pleased to see Gethin having a go.

"Because they used to build houses out of earth?"

Gethin heard a burst of giggles spreading through the class and felt himself blush. He'd made a fool of himself.

"Correct. Well done you," said Mr Davies, turning to the lot who were laughing. "So you can all stop making that silly noise."

The giggling quietened down and Mr Davies continued.

"In former times, many people were too poor to build stone houses, so they made their homes out of earth or clay."

"What? Like mud huts?" asked a girl called Lowri, who

always said stupid things on purpose. Everyone laughed again.

"Not exactly, Lowri. We'll be taking a trip to St Fagan's – the National Museum of History – before Christmas. You'll see an earth house then. So the full, proper meaning of Pontypridd is 'Y bont ar bwys y tŷ pridd' – 'the bridge by the earth house'. But of course the earth house is long gone by now."

"They still live in mud huts in Cilfynydd," said Lowri, throwing a sly glance in Gethin's direction. Everyone laughed again – apart from Caitlin. Gethin wanted to sink into his seat and disappear from view. Cilfynydd. That was the part of Pontypridd where he lived.

"Yng Nghilfynydd," corrected Mr Davies. "That's the correct way to say 'in Cilfynydd'. And the last time I looked, they were brick houses. So where do you live, Lowri? Trallwn, is it?"

"Best place in Ponty, sir," answered Lowri, smiling.

"Any idea what the name means?"

"Something cool, I bet."

"I'm not sure about cool. Trallwn means a wet, muddy place."

The class burst into laughter once more, and it was Lowri's turn to look uncomfortable. She didn't say a word after that, and Mr Davies was able to get on with the lesson.

The subject was place names and how they could bring the past alive, if you understood their meaning. Two examples struck Gethin. The first was 'Twyn yr Odyn'. 'Twyn' meant hillock, and an 'odyn' was a kiln to burn limestone to make lime, which was used like fertiliser on fields and as whitewash on the walls of houses: 'Limestone-kiln hillock'. The second was 'Tonypandy'. 'Ton' was a local name for a field, and 'pandy' was a place to wash and thicken wool, before it was treated: 'Wool-washery field'.

Then Mr Davies started talking about how place names often described local geography. There were lots of memorable ones in the area, like Nantgarw (Rugged brook or ravine) and Rhydfelen (Yellow ford). But Gethin's favourite example was the name of a farm – Nyth Brân, which meant Crow's Nest.

This had been the home of the famous runner, Gruffydd Morgan – or Guto, as everyone called him – who'd lived some three hundred years ago. From when he was a child, local people had spoken in awe of Guto's speed and claimed all sorts of amazing things about him – that he could chase and catch wild animals, or run to take a message to the nearest town and be home before the kettle boiled. Whatever the truth of these tales, it was obvious that Guto really was a very fast runner and, when he was older, he'd won race after race.

Gethin was all ears now. As the poster of Mo Farah on his bedroom wall proved, he was mad about anything to do with running. Though he wasn't much of a runner himself –he'd been ill a lot when he was younger so his mam didn't think it was a good idea – he was quite an expert when it came to world records and athletes' training methods.

"Caitlin Derbyshire, I hope that's not a mobile phone you're holding under the desk," said Mr Davies, loudly.

Gethin had been so caught up in the story of Guto Nyth Brân that he jumped in his seat. Mr Davies's voice had sounded sharper than usual.

"Just Googling Guto Nyth Brân, sir," explained Caitlin, putting her phone aside at once.

"I'm glad to know you're so keen, but I don't want to see that phone again during this lesson."

"Sorry, sir," said Caitlin, realising at once that he meant it.

Then Mr Davies asked everyone to find out more about Guto Nyth Brân for homework – a task Gethin was looking forward to already.

After the class he was dying to know what Caitlin had found out about Guto Nyth Brân.

But when he asked her she replied, "You're so sweet!" as if she was speaking to a little child, before showing him her phone. On it were pictures of witches, pumpkins and ghosts. Nothing at all to do with the runner.

"I was getting ideas for my Hallowe'en party," explained Caitlin.

Gethin couldn't believe his ears.

"So you lied to Mr Davies," he said.

"Course I did. Everyone tells lies sometimes. Don't you?" she asked, challenging him with a wide smile.

Gethin had told his mam a lie this morning, of course. But that was different, somehow. He thought hard before answering – so hard he didn't notice Caitlin drifting away to join her friends.

"Yes, I do, sometimes. When I have to," he said at last. But there was no one there to hear him. *Maybe Caitlin's lost interest in me already,* he thought. *I don't blame her.*

4

It all happened so quickly. Gethin hit the ground before he realised he'd been tripped. But once he saw Cai standing over him, cracking up with laughter, he knew exactly what had happened.

"Loser," said Cai, in a menacingly quiet voice, before jogging over to Nathan, who was leaning against the Science block wall and staring across the yard, his eyes taking in everything and everyone.

Gethin wasn't sure which was worse – the fact that Cai had picked on him; or the obvious sympathy of the Tri Trist – the Sad Three – who were standing nearby. *Perhaps I really am a loser*, he thought, before getting up off the ground and trying to behave as if nothing had happened.

He saw the Tri Trist discussing something between them and looking over in his direction. Then, a little hesitantly, they began to walk towards him. But before they reached him, someone else came striding in his direction. Caitlin. There was nothing hesitant about her as she lifted a hand to shoo the boys away, as if they were nothing more than pesky pigeons.

"You're not friends with them, I hope?" she said.

"No," said Gethin, promptly.

"Good. They're such nerds."

"I know," he agreed, feeling a little uncomfortable, especially as the boys were within earshot and were staring over at them.

Then Caitlin passed him something: a card with a picture of a big pumpkin on it.

"What's this?" asked Gethin.

"Invitation to my Hallowe'en party, silly," explained Caitlin.

"You're inviting *me*?" said Gethin, stunned, and he felt himself blush. Again. He really had to stop blushing all the time. It was so embarrassing.

"Yes. You. Is there any reason why I shouldn't?" teased Caitlin.

"No, I don't think so," answered Gethin.

Caitlin laughed. "You're really funny, you know that?"

"Am I?" Gethin had never thought of himself as being funny.

"So – are you going to come, or not?" asked Caitlin, glancing over in Nathan's direction. Nathan's sharp eyes were fixed on the two of them, taking an obvious interest in the conversation.

"I'll have to ask Mam first," said Gethin. "But I'm sure there'll be no problem," he added quickly.

"Don't forget to wear fancy dress, or you won't be allowed in the house," warned Caitlin, with a cheeky smile.

Then she turned on her heel, leaving Gethin to stare at the invitation in his hand. If he'd looked up, he'd have seen Caitlin flouncing past Nathan and Cai with her head held high. And he'd have seen Nathan watching her every step.

But Gethin was still looking at the invitation. Caitlin hadn't lost interest in him after all. Quite the opposite. She'd invited him to her party!

The bell went. Gethin put the invitation in his bag – carefully, so as not to crease it – and, ignoring the Tri Trist, he entered the Science block.

5

"Of course you can go!" said Gethin's mam, obviously delighted for him. She was always going on about Gethin making new friends.

"I'll make you a fancy-dress costume, if you like. I can make something much better than that plastic rubbish they sell in shops."

Gethin wasn't too sure about this and he tried to suggest, tactfully, that his costume had to be a proper one, not something thrown together. Big mistake, of course, as his mam reminded him, indignantly, that she was an old hand at the sewing machine and knew exactly what she was doing.

Before she could get stuck in to a full-on lecture, Gethin escaped to his bedroom. He still couldn't believe that Caitlin had invited him to the party, and by now he'd started to worry that the whole thing was some kind of cruel trick. Had she done it to make a fool of him?

He was working himself up by overthinking things, as usual. Gethin was always worried about something, forever creating stories in his mind. When he was little, he used to imagine meeting his dad – though he'd left his mam while she was expecting Gethin and hadn't been in touch since. Gethin had created a clear picture of him in his mind: a tall man, fit, with a mop of black hair that was starting to go grey, and a kind smile. Once, one Saturday afternoon, he persuaded himself that his dad was right outside the house, waiting for Gethin to come and play football with him in the park. And if his mam hadn't caught him going out the door, he would have waited there for ever, watching out for his dad. In vain, of course.

To try to quieten his anxious thoughts, Gethin decided to clean his pet's home – his pet being a small gecko called Emil. Emil wasn't a common gecko but a leopard gecko – a little creature whose skin was coloured brightly with orange, chocolate and white. Gethin was lucky to own him – his mam would never have agreed to him having Emil at all, if they hadn't had to move so suddenly to live with Gransha.

It'd been Gransha who'd chosen the gecko's name. At first, the little creature had had mad moments where he'd race about in his new glass home like a wild thing, shaking his head from side to side. Gransha said the gecko reminded him of one of his biggest heroes, the runner from the Czech Republic called Emil Zátopek, who'd been really famous when Gransha was a young man. In fact, this was the only thing that Gethin and his tad-cu had in common – their love of athletics.

In a painfully exact and conscientious way, Gethin placed fresh, shredded paper at the bottom of the rectangular glass tank. People usually used sand, but some young geckos ate sand until they were old enough to know better. Gethin didn't want to take that risk, so shredded paper would have to do for the time being.

After he'd cleaned the tank, it was time to feed Emil. Usually, Emil would get a few mealworms, but as Gethin felt today was a special occasion, he gave him a live cricket – an insect similar to a grasshopper.

Then, for just a moment, Gethin froze in horror as an image flashed across his mind – an image of him as the cricket and Nathan as the gecko.

Gethin switched off the tank's light and turned his back. Suddenly, he didn't want to see what was about to happen.

Instead, he looked at the poster on his wall. Mo Farah was smiling at him, as ever, and Gethin felt a little better. He thought about Caitlin's smile, and the invitation, and then he decided to give her a present – not some nickel-and-dime trinket that any fool could buy in a shop, but a proper present, made especially for her. He remembered the little box he'd made in Technology at his old school. If he were to carve Caitlin's name on the lid of the box and put a bit of shine on the wood, it would make a great present.

When he came down to the kitchen his mam was in a good mood – such a good mood that she'd ordered pizza all round. This was something of an exception – as was the fact that Gransha was in the kitchen too. And the two of them were drinking a can of beer and speaking nicely to each other.

"*What's all this I hear about a party?*" asked his tad-cu, in English. He couldn't speak Welsh – only one or two words, although he could understand a lot more than he let on, which was why Gethin didn't usually bother changing to English when talking to him.

Gethin blushed, despite having promised himself he

wouldn't do it again. The question had come so unexpectedly, he'd been taken by surprise.

"*Leave him be. You're making him blush, look*," warned his mam.

Gransha said no more about it but he couldn't help winking at Gethin while Helen's back was turned.

The pizza came. Gethin ate every piece. He was starving. He ate Gransha's last piece too, and his mam's.

"Perhaps you're growing," said his mam, pleased.

I hope so, thought Gethin. It was two months now since he'd turned thirteen, and he still wasn't one and a half metres tall.

As everyone was in such a good mood, Gethin suggested that they play Monopoly. Usually, his mam would make excuses not to, but she agreed at once. She even laughed quite a lot as they played, and Gethin was delighted to see how young and pretty she looked when she was happy.

Another great surprise came when it turned out Gransha knew quite a lot about Guto Nyth Brân.

"*Course I do. Local boy he was, see*," he explained, launching into the story of Guto's last ever race. Guto was so famous for running so fast that no one wanted to compete against him – until 1737, when a man called Prince challenged him for a prize of a thousand guineas, which was a little over a thousand pounds: a huge sum in those days. Guto won, but he paid a frightening price. Straight after crossing the finishing line, Guto had collapsed and died.

At this, a shiver coursed through Gethin's body. It felt like someone had opened the kitchen door and let in a cold gust of wind. Meanwhile, the Monopoly game continued, and Gransha and Gethin's mam opened another can of beer and were smiling cheerfully at each other. But the story of Guto had dampened Gethin's enthusiasm. All he could think about now was the young runner – lying, dead, on the ground.

Gransha won the game. Gethin's mam planted a huge kiss on his check – and Gethin felt a lump in his throat, but he wasn't sure why.

6

Gethin was proud of himself – and that didn't happen often. He'd just been given permission to join the Technology Club after school to finish Caitlin's present. He hadn't given any details about the box, just said he wanted to finish a 'project'.

So now he had five minutes for a bit of fresh air before the bell went for the first lesson. Stepping into the school yard, he noticed how bright everything looked in the low light of the autumn sun: the purple stripe across one of the buildings, the multicoloured, shimmering leaves of the trees in the distance, the silver-foil chewing gum packet that someone had dropped on the ground and the gleam of the teachers' cars in the car park near the entrance. It was as if the world had been washed clean.

Then, "Gethin. That's your name, yeah?" said a voice from behind him. A boy's voice, hovering within a note or two of a man's. Nathan's voice.

Gethin turned to face him.

"Yeah."

"You're friends with Caitlin," he went on.

Something deep in Gethin's bones told him to be on guard, to watch what he said, but before he knew what he was doing, he was answering.

"Yes, I am. I'm going to her party."

"What party?"

"A Hallowe'en party. At her house."

It was obvious from his surprised expression that Nathan hadn't been invited. Perhaps he'd be offended? Gethin hoped not.

Nathan was eyeing him carefully now, as if he was weighing him up. "I want you to do me a favour," he said.

Favour? Nathan Jenkins was asking *him* – the invisible Gethin Tanner – to do him a favour?

"If you do it, I'll make sure Cai stops picking on you."

Gethin couldn't believe his ears. Maybe his luck was turning, at last. Maybe things were starting to go his way.

"Of course," answered Gethin, eagerly.

Then Nathan explained. He wanted Gethin to find out what kind of music Caitlin was into. What her interests and hobbies were, her favourite films and TV programmes, all that kind of thing.

"I want to buy her a birthday present," said Nathan.

Gethin stared at him in astonishment. "Why?" he asked, in a voice that was little more than a whisper, because in truth he already knew the answer.

"Why d'you think?" Nathan grinned, then walked away.

Gethin's heart sank to his shoes. Nathan fancied Caitlin. No two ways about it. The bell went, but Gethin was frozen to the spot. And for the first time since he'd started at his new school, he was late for the next lesson.

~

Double French. And though Gethin was pretty good at the subject, Mademoiselle Guillemin might as well have been talking Mandarin for all the notice he took today. Nathan's voice was echoing in his head, and the fact that he was using him to get close to Caitlin weighed in his stomach like a stone.

Straight after lunchtime bell, Gethin headed behind the school for the furthest corner of the rugby pitch. This is where he came – fairly often, in fact – to get away from everyone and everything. Putting his coat down, he sat on it. Then he looked up and saw that the sun was now hiding behind the clouds.

He pulled his lunch box out of his bag and bit, listlessly, into a cheese sandwich. Mademoiselle Guillemin had asked him if anything was wrong. He'd done his best to smile at her and tell her everything was fine.

But, of course, everything *wasn't* fine. Not by a long shot. The cheese sandwich began to turn in his stomach and he put the rest of it back in the box. He'd need to remember to throw it in the bin – if he took it home uneaten his mam would nag at him.

If Gethin had been brave enough, he'd have told Caitlin everything. And if he'd been crafty enough, he'd have asked

Caitlin what she liked then told the opposite to Nathan. But Nathan wasn't stupid. He'd soon realise he'd been duped. Gethin sighed. What choice did he have, when it came down to it? Having Cai as an enemy was bad enough. But having Nathan as an enemy . . . that would be a hundred times worse.

~

If Gethin had trouble concentrating in French, he was completely hopeless by afternoon lessons, even Geography. Miss Thompson was his favourite teacher, along with Mr Davies Cymraeg. This term they were learning about what caused worldwide climate change, and its effects. Although Gethin found the subject pretty alarming – especially at night, when he couldn't sleep for worrying – he enjoyed the lessons. But today, everything Miss Thompson said just made him feel even more depressed.

The last bell went and the class burst headlong from the classroom and into the corridor. But unlike the rest, who were stampeding towards the school gates, Caitlin was standing outside the door, waiting for him.

"I've bought myself a lush fancy dress for the party. What are you coming as?" she bubbled happily. Gethin had no idea what to say. He knew his mam was up to something on the sewing machine, but she was keeping the outfit a close secret. He definitely wasn't going to admit to that, though. Not to Caitlin.

"I'm not saying."

"Ooh – surprise, yeah?" laughed Caitlin. Then, "I'm really glad you can come to the party," she added.

Her kind words made this even harder. Why did she have to be so lovely?

Gethin cleared his throat. "Come on. Let's head for the bus."

And they walked he questioned her about her favourite music and TV programmes, what she liked doing, her interests and hobbies – exactly as Nathan had asked him to. When they got to the bus stop, Gethin said goodbye.

"Why? You not going home?" asked Caitlin.

"No. I'm doing something after school," he answered.

"I know why you were asking all those questions," said Caitlin.

Gethin looked down to hide his guilty expression. Had she somehow discovered the truth?

"You're so sweet. But you don't have to give me a present. You know that, right?" she went on, smiling, before climbing on to the bus. The stone in Gethin's stomach grew even heavier. This was so unfair! But he should've known by now that life wasn't fair. After all, his mam was always telling him so.

~

Neatly and with great care, Gethin carved Caitlin's name on to the box's lid and polished up the wood. It looked great, and he felt sure Caitlin would be thrilled. That was the important thing. He knew fine well that he wasn't tall, good-looking or mature enough to be her boyfriend. But even if she was unwise enough to go out with Nathan, there was no reason why she and Gethin couldn't be friends.

As he approached the school gates he saw a familiar, menacing figure standing there, even though school had finished two hours ago.

"Where you been?" spat Nathan. "I've been waiting for you."

"Sorry, I didn't know. I was in Technology Club," explained Gethin, not saying why.

"Tell me what you've found out."

This wasn't a question – it was an order. And though Gethin knew that he'd regret it in the end, he told him everything. Nathan listened carefully, devouring every detail.

When Gethin had finished, Nathan stared at him, thoughtfully. His eyes were almost as penetrating as Caitlin's. Gethin gripped his bag, tightly.

Big mistake.

"What you got in your bag?"

"Nothing."

Before he knew it, Nathan had torn the bag out of his hands. He rummaged inside it and pulled out the present. Then he stared at it intently, turning it in his hands.

"Perfect," Nathan said at last, smiling. His smile was even more terrifying than his frown. "I think I'll give this to Caitlin myself." Holding on to the wooden box, he threw Gethin's bag to the ground.

"One more thing," he went on. "I need you to keep away from Caitlin from now on, OK?"

Again, this was an order, not a question. Nathan turned

on his heel without bothering to hear Gethin's answer.

No, it's *not* OK! That's what Gethin wanted to shout, right in his face. But, of course, he didn't. He didn't say a thing. He stood there for ages, staring into the distance like a wordless wimp, even after it began chucking it down with rain.

7

"Of course you're going – especially after I've gone to the trouble of making you a special costume!" thundered Gethin's mam.

He'd just told her he wasn't going to Caitlin's party after all, because he felt ill. And his mam was fuming. Usually, she was full of sympathy when he wasn't well – but not this time. He tried again.

"But I feel really ill, Mam."

"You're nervous – that's all. You'll be fine once you're there."

"But Ma-am, you don't understand . . ."

"You're going, and that's the end of it."

Gethin knew better than to carry on arguing, or to tell her the truth about Nathan's threats. She'd go nuts and kick up an almighty fuss at school. Gethin's stomach was seething for real by now. Perhaps he could make himself sick in the toilet; perhaps his mam would let him stay home then . . .

"Right. No more nonsense. Try your costume on."

His mam threw the fancy dress on Gethin's bed before leaving the room and slamming the door shut behind her.

Lying on the bed was a long, green cape. Under the cape was a simple jacket, a waistcoat and a pair of trousers – every one of them bright yellow. And hanging beneath the trousers – which looked too short, even for Gethin – were two very strange things: a pair of rubber slippers with curly fur on them. Even worse, at the top sat a shaggy brown wig – and attached to the wig were two huge, slightly pointed ears. He realised in a flash what his mam's costume was. Not Dracula. Not a zombie. Not even Darth Vader – but a Hobbit . . .

A Hobbit! How could his mam be so *stupid*? A Hobbit wasn't frightening at all – and everyone knew that frightening people was the whole point of Hallowe'en. Even worse than that, Hobbits were famous for being small. Perhaps his mam hadn't realised how sensitive Gethin was about his height – or *lack* of height, more like.

He sighed, deeply, and tried the costume on. It fitted perfectly, worse luck. He went to the bathroom to look at himself in the mirror. In his yellow outfit and green cloak he looked like a daffodil. Or a canary. One thing was for sure – he didn't look cool.

Head down, Gethin walked into his mam's bedroom. She stared at him, wordlessly. Then a little smile spread across her face.

"Not bad at all, though I say so myself."

For once, Gethin couldn't enjoy seeing his mam smile. He knew he ought to say thank you for all her hard work, but the words refused to come.

~

At least it's dark in Caitlin's house, thought Gethin as he helped himself to a second glass of bright purple pop in the kitchen.

He could hear everyone screaming and laughing in the next room, even through the big plastic ears stuck to the wig that was making his head itch like crazy. Candle-light lit the downstairs rooms – some in hollowed-out pumpkins and some on saucers. Gethin's mam would've had a fit if she'd seen them – she'd have found it all far too dangerous.

"*Here's* where you're hiding!" cried Caitlin, bursting into the kitchen. She was dressed as a witch – the prettiest witch Gethin had ever seen.

"Your costume's really great. It must've taken your mam ages," she added.

"Yes – it did," answered Gethin, as enthusiastically as he could.

"Thanks for the present. It was . . . *interesting*."

It was obvious from the way she said 'interesting' that Caitlin wasn't that keen on the present – which had been a vinyl record, since she'd got a turntable for her birthday, or a 'proper record player' as her father insisted on calling it. The local shop hadn't sold anything by Caitlin's favourite band, so Gethin had had to buy another one, at random, and he'd obviously got it wrong.

He took another gulp of pop before he said anything else he'd regret . . . like he'd had a much better gift for her but Nathan had stolen it from him. His stomach churned, and not because of the pop. He couldn't help imagining Caitlin's reaction to his real present.

"Come on. We're going out."

"Out? Why?" asked Gethin. The last thing he wanted was to leave Caitlin's house in his Hobbit costume.

"Trick or treating, of course," laughed Caitlin. But Gethin didn't feel like laughing. What if someone saw him and told Nathan?

~

Most of Caitlin's neighbours answered their doors, fair play to them, and they'd bought loads of sweets – enough for the whole gang: Gethin and Caitlin; Caitlin's best friends from the street, Holly and Molly (who were also dressed as witches); Molly's brothers Joshua and Tyler and three girls from school – Ffion, Natalie and Bethan. Caitlin's mam had given them two bags as big as sacks to collect the sweets, so they could share the sugary treasure out equally when they got back to the house.

Only Tyler, Molly's four-year-old little brother, took any notice of Gethin – apart from Caitlin, of course. Tyler stared up at Gethin with round, awe-struck eyes as they tramped the streets – it was obvious that the little boy thought he was trick or treating with a real Hobbit.

Suddenly, an ear-splitting clap thundered, echoing, between the houses. *BANG!* As the firework exploded its brief flash lit up the brick buildings. The next moment, Gethin felt a little hand clutching his. Tyler was at his side, staring up at him with big, frightened eyes.

BANG! Another one. Who was letting them off? Gethin turned and made out half a dozen zombies, lurking in the shadows at the far end of the street. One huge zombie seemed to be leading them – behind him trailed a smaller phantom, more frightening than all the rest, somehow, despite its pitiful size. Gethin shivered as he realised that the big, tall zombie was none other than Nathan Jenkins and that the sinister squirt at his side was Cai Thomas. Had Nathan recognised Caitlin? More importantly, had Nathan recognised *him*?

Then Tyler began to cry, so Gethin whispered to him that everything was all right, they were only fireworks. Then he put his hand on his shoulder to comfort the little boy, whisking the green cloak aside as he did so. At that moment, Nathan stalked away, leading his gang from the scene. Coincidence, of course. But to little Tyler, it'd looked as if Gethin had magicked them away by lifting his hand and whispering a special spell.

"The Hobbit saved us from the monsters!" he called out, in wonder.

Everyone laughed. Tyler protested, insisting that the Hobbit really was magic, but this made them all laugh even harder. And Gethin felt a warm wave of relief flow over him as he watched Nathan and his devilish gang disappear from sight.

~

Half an hour later everyone was starting to tire, especially Tyler, who was whining to his sister and dragging his feet. What's more, the two trick-or-treat bags were overflowing with sweets by now, so they all decided to call it a day and head back to the house. This was a big relief for Gethin because walking in his Hobbit slippers was making his feet hurt.

"I'm just going to take these stupid things off," he said to Caitlin. "You lot go ahead – Tyler needs to get home to bed."

"OK. Don't be long."

Gethin sat down on a low wall and watched them head off down the street. Then he looked down at the town and all its lights, glittering like hundreds of Hallowe'en candles. He yanked at his rubber slippers but, strangely, they wouldn't come off. It was as if they'd been glued to his feet. There was nothing for it, then, but to follow the others back to Caitlin's, still wearing his stupid footwear.

Gethin didn't notice the menacing shadow, lurking in a narrow lane that led up the slope from the street – until it was too late. An arm shot out of the darkness and dragged him savagely into the pitch-black alley.

"Trick or treat?" croaked a harsh, familiar voice. A voice to strike fear into the dead. Nathan's voice.

A firework lit the sky with a flash of gold and white, and Gethin saw something shining in Nathan's hand. A *knife*? He wasn't going to hang about to find out. With a swift, side-stepping leap he dislodged Nathan's hand and darted past him, running hell for leather up the narrow, dark lane.

No one had expected this, including Gethin himself. Nathan stood stock still for a few moments before hurling himself after him, the other zombies tailing him like maddened, howling hounds.

Gethin climbed higher and higher, though the steep lane was sucking every ounce of his energy. In no time, everything was hurting – his lungs, his legs, his feet. His head was rocking from side to side like a ragdoll and his mouth was wide open, gulping down cold air. *Just like Emil Zátopek*, he thought, wishing Gransha could see him now.

But there was no time to think, no time for anything but escape. Gethin reached the end of the lane and realised he was almost at the top of the hill. Turning swiftly, he saw Nathan battling up the slope towards him. Cai was on his heels. And the rest were far behind.

Gethin forced his legs to move again. He had to keep going. Turning right he hit a path that led across a field towards the darkness of a wood, and he sprinted headlong down it. If only he could reach the trees in time, perhaps he'd have a chance to hide.

Now he was running across wet ground and he realised, in terror, that he was slowing and that the ground felt like sticky treacle – just like his nightmare. This was what it meant, then. Nathan was the beast. And he was going to tear him to pieces. Only a few seconds separated him and Nathan now. *Maybe I should just give up*, he thought. *Stand still. Accept the inevitable.*

But as Nathan took his last, fateful paces towards Gethin, he tripped over an old, rotten log and fell to the ground. This was another, unexpected reprieve and, from somewhere, Gethin found the strength to keep pumping his now-shaking legs. Right, left. Right, left. Right, left.

Before long, Gethin had reached the wood. Throwing

himself over the stile he limped along a narrow path between trees. Luckily for Gethin, the path headed downwards, so he could speed up a bit. He could hear Nathan and Cai somewhere behind him, threatening him, their furious swearwords crackling through the night air.

Instinctively, he dodged off the path and dragged himself through undergrowth until he burst into a clearing encircled by broad oak trees, like a dark room right in the middle of the wood – just the place to hide. As Gethin tried to control his breathing, he realised how very tight his chest felt – as tight as if someone had encased him in a steel belt. The pain was even worse than when he awoke from the nightmare. The world about him shrank down to a tiny point, so that it was only Gethin. Only Gethin, and his pain.

The last thing he saw as he collapsed to the ground were the stars between the branches of the oaks. Shining. Like Caitlin's eyes.

And then everything went black.

PART 2

8

The next thing Gethin heard was the cawing of crows. Opening his eyes he saw two big, black carrion crows staring down at him from one of the encircling oak trees. He must have lain here through the night. In the weak, morning light, the trees looked smaller than they had last night. Staring up through the branches he saw a whole flock of crows, flying high up in the sky. From here, they looked like black, winged spiders. A shiver coursed down his spine. He hated spiders.

Gethin struggled up, on to his feet. Every part of his body was hurting but, strangely, he didn't feel cold. He tried to walk, and after a step or two he realised, to his surprise, that his legs weren't stiff at all. So he headed home, though he wasn't sure exactly which way to go. The wood was so thick that he couldn't see much more than a couple of metres in front of him; it was much thicker than it'd seemed last night.

At last Gethin reached the edge of the wood. In no time he'd see Pontypridd below him, and he'd know exactly where he was and how to get home. His heart sank as he realised that everyone would be worried sick about him by now. He must have spoiled Caitlin's party. And what about his mam?

Would she be angry, or glad to see him? Or both?

All of a sudden, the quarrelling, cawing sound of the crows quietened. Everything went quiet. Too quiet. As Gethin stared down over the edge of the hill towards town, he realised why.

Pontypridd had disappeared.

He rubbed his eyes. This wasn't possible. He looked again. Where, a few hours ago, there'd been a busy town, now there were a handful of cottages, a few fields, and woods. Downriver, he saw a wooden bridge. There was no sign of William Edwards's arched, stone bridge – one of Pontypridd's most famous landmarks. And it was the same on the far side of the valley: nothing but fields and a few small, white buildings, peppering the hills. Where on earth was he?

Before he could answer this question he heard a scream from behind him. Spinning around, he saw someone – or something – darting away, unnaturally fast, like some alien creature in a horror film. Gethin screamed too and legged it in the opposite direction – back into the trees. But, despite his fear, Gethin couldn't help noticing how easily he could run.

After a few minutes' hard sprinting, Gethin slowed. He didn't want to venture further into the depths of the dark, endless wood and risk getting lost. Stumbling into a thick cluster of young trees, he sat down on a large stone in the middle of them. This would do for a hiding place, for now. And, as he got his breath back, he realised that his lungs didn't hurt at all. What a great feeling! He smiled, until he heard someone – or something – approaching. Had the alien creature returned? Maybe Gethin wasn't on Earth at all. Maybe he'd, somehow, materialised in another dimension, on a distant planet.

But it wasn't an alien walking towards him but a young boy, about the same age as Gethin himself. He was no normal boy, however. His clothes looked really old-fashioned, for a start. He was barefoot and his unwashed black hair was all over the place – in fact, he looked as if he hadn't been near a bath or shower for months. Was he some sort of spirit?

As he drew closer, the boy made the sign of the cross with his hands, over and over, mumbling something that sounded like a prayer or a rhyme. *He's even more afraid of me than I am of him*, Gethin realised.

"Tawninmarwtadawetwsygwirychchifendithymamaynmy ndfelsglemin!"

As the words bubbled from the boy's mouth in a long, garbled stream, Gethin stared at him in astonishment, not understanding a word. Then the boy took a deep breath and spoke more slowly.

"Tawn i'n marw! Tada wetws y gwir! Ych chi Fendith y Mama yn mynd fel sglemin!"

He was speaking Welsh! But it was a very strange Welsh – definitely different to anything Gethin had heard before. As he tried to guess what the words meant, he felt a switch flip in his head and everything fell into place. The boy was saying: "Wel, yr argoel fawr! Dwedodd Dad y gwir! Y'ch chi dylwyth teg mor gyflym ag ystlum!"

In other words, "Well, blow me down! Dad was telling the truth! You tylwyth teg are as fast as bats!"

The tylwyth teg were the fairy folk. What did he mean by that? Then Gethin realised. He was still wearing his Hobbit outfit. The boy thought he was one of the tylwyth teg! Suddenly, the boy fell to his knees and bowed his head. In his odd-sounding Welsh, he went on,

"Forgive me. I shouldn't have greeted you without your leave. I am at your service."

It was obvious that he believed in the tylwyth teg, and that he had a lot of respect for them. He was looking at Gethin expectantly, from the corner of his eye. Gethin decided not to explain that he was just a boy . . . for now, at least. He cleared his throat.

"Where am I?"

"The woods of Craig-yr-hesg. Parish of Llanwynno. Morgannwg."

Exactly where he'd been before, then, though this was a pretty strange way of describing the place. *Why doesn't he just say 'Pontypridd'?* wondered Gethin.

"And what's the date?"

"Dydd Calan Gaea, 1713."

At this, Gethin's throat went dry as a bone. All Saints' Day – the day after Hallowe'en – 1713! Somehow, he'd travelled over three hundred years into the past! No wonder the boy hadn't named the town – Pontypridd hadn't even existed at this point. And the stone bridge it was named after hadn't been built yet either.

The boy got up and stepped towards him. *That's strange*, thought Gethin. He was exactly the same height as Gethin, to the centimetre. But though he was short he stood straight and square and introduced himself in a steady, formal voice:

"Gruffydd Morgan. But everybody calls me Guto. Guto Nyth Brân."

9

Gethin was beginning to worry that Guto would never return and that he'd be lost in the woods for ever. Guto had left him here, promising to come back with food and clothes. How long ago had that been? Two hours? Three? Somehow, every minute felt like an hour and every hour like a minute.

At last Gethin heard someone approaching. Then he saw Guto striding towards him. Behind him were three other boys, who were staring at him with eyes like saucers. Guto introduced them, one by one.

"I've brought my best friends to meet you. Ifan Blaenhenwysg, Dafydd Penrhiwgwynt and Siencyn Hafod Ucha."

The boys smiled at him, shyly. They looked a bit odd, as odd as their weird names. They were probably called after their home farms, thought Gethin, just like Guto. There was something very familiar about them. Then Gethin realised why. They were just like those three outsiders, the Tri Trist!

"And . . . your good self?" asked Guto.

"Call me Gethin."

"Gethin," breathed all four of them, in wonder.

Then Guto handed him a linen cloth. Wrapped inside it was a piece of flat, hard bread.

"Unleavened bread. Not much of a feast, I'm a-feared, Gethin."

Gethin wasn't sure what 'unleavened' meant, but he guessed it was a word to describe bread that hadn't risen, because it looked more like a naan or a pitta bread than a normal loaf. He tore a piece off and chewed on it. It was pretty tough and dry, but it was better than nothing and he was starving. He took another piece and stuffed it into his mouth.

"Here be clothing," added Guto, passing him a sack. The clothes inside it looked even more ragged than the ones Guto and the rest were wearing. But Gethin tried to smile, so as not to look ungrateful.

Then, telling the boys to stay where they were, Gethin ducked behind a tree to get changed – not wanting them to realise that the tylwyth teg outfit was fancy dress. As he pulled on the ragged clothes, a damp, muggy smell rose from them, and the material felt rough and itched even worse than the stupid wig he was still wearing. He tore it off his head and yanked hard at his slippers, and this time they came off with no trouble.

But as he stuffed the fancy dress in the bag, pain shot through him. Suddenly, the bread in his stomach felt heavy as a stone, as if it was battling against his body.

By the time he'd staggered back to the boys, Gethin was in agony. He saw their eyes grow wide in alarm at the sight of his pale face but, before he could explain that something was badly wrong, the world began to spin about him. The boys' anxious voices faded into the distance and Gethin fainted on the spot, for the second time in less than twelve hours.

~

As he rested, hidden beneath a pile of straw in the cowshed, Gethin relived the exhausting journey from the wood to Nyth Brân in his mind. He hoped this would keep him awake – because something, deep in his bones, was telling him not to fall asleep, despite the fact that his eyelids were really heavy.

Back in the woods, Guto and his friends had managed to lift then half support, half carry him every step of the way here – the longest two miles Gethin had ever known. The country lanes were no more than rough, muddy paths and, apart from the half a dozen farms and cottages that Guto had pointed out on the way, there were no buildings anywhere. The only time they'd seen a person coming towards them, the boys had dodged behind a hedge to hide before staggering on their way once more when the coast was clear.

As they'd approached Nyth Brân, Gethin had started to feel his mind and body slipping away again, so he'd done his best to stay awake by counting his steps – until he reached a hundred and the numbers began to run together and become muddled. Then he sang the nursery rhyme, 'Mi Welais Jac y Do', to himself, quietly, over and over, before he became so confused he couldn't remember the order of the lines.

The whole time, Guto had been gabbling at the top of his voice to try to lift Gethin's spirits, so, desperate not to drift off, Gethin had kept his mind busy by trying to work out exactly how Guto and the others' Welsh was different to his.

It wasn't just that their Welsh sounded really old, but it sounded, well, different. Some letters seemed to 'harden', so a 'd' could become a 't', for example. They also had a strange way of pronouncing the long 'ah' sound, so rather than rhyming with 'char' or 'far', it rhymed with 'chair' or 'fair'. And it wasn't only the sound – a lot of the actual words were ones he'd never heard before, and even the order they came in a sentence was sometimes different. So 'she walked' came out as something like 'walketh she'.

All this kept Gethin so busy that, before he knew it, they'd arrived at Nyth Brân farm.

But they hadn't gone into the house. They hid behind a hedge again, until it got dark. For obvious reasons, Guto didn't want his parents knowing he'd brought a member of the tylwyth teg home with him.

Back in the cowshed, Gethin squirmed under the straw. The pain was unbearable by now and had spread from his stomach to the rest of his body. He felt as if he was melting, like ice cream that'd been out of the freezer for too long.

Gethin opened his eyes to see Caitlin standing over him. Then his mam. And Gransha. But he knew they weren't really there. Another face swam into view – a face that was full of anguish – Guto's.

"Help me," whispered Gethin, "before it's too late."

~

The night was as black as pitch and the roaring wind was poking cold, sly fingers through the woollen blanket that covered him. But Gethin hardly noticed, he was so weak. As the wind tired and faded before getting up again, Gethin could hear Guto's father's heavy breathing as he carried him on his back through the darkness, over fields and through woods, crossing Llwyncelyn brook and the Rhondda Fach river and climbing the hill on the other side.

Gethin's desperate words in the cowshed had spurred Guto on to fetch his parents. And when they'd seen him writhing in pain, they'd decided to trek to the ancient, holy spring nearby, in hopes of curing Gethin – who was, by now, losing consciousness.

At last they reached the brow of the hill. The wind was howling even more furiously up here. Gethin bounced on Guto's father's back as he rushed with him towards the spring, then he felt himself being tenderly laid down.

"Leave us not, my beautiful boy," begged Guto's father.

Gethin was trying his hardest not to fall asleep. Time felt confused. Seconds rushed past without him realising and then, suddenly, he'd be completely in the present, every nerve in his body tingling – aware of the blanket's wool itching his skin; a flash of lightning; the little wax figure wearing a piece of Gethin's clothing that Guto's father had placed next to the spring; the words of his earnest prayer, begging the Virgin Mary to cure Gethin; the sour taste of the spring water and then the cold when his head was pushed underwater, water so cold that it burned.

When Gethin lifted his head from the spring, all his

senses seemed to explode. He could see everything about him clearly, despite the darkness. And he could hear the chatter of the Rhondda Fach far below and the whisper of the Rhondda Fawr on the other side of the hill, despite the moans and cries of the wind. He felt the strength flowing back into his body, as if some mad scientist had injected him with magic potion. But as the world around him came to life, he felt the world he'd left, the modern Pontypridd, retreat.

Then came another bout of exhaustion. But this exhaustion was different. He wasn't afraid to fall asleep this time, because he knew now that he was safe.

10

Gethin awoke to see two little girls, staring at him with round eyes. They were as alike as peas in a pod: rosy cheeks, big blue eyes and curly black hair. A moment later, they'd turned on their heels and disappeared from view. Gethin heard their voices shouting:

"Mam! Mam! The boy's awake!"

Gethin got up, rubbing his head to dislodge the pieces of straw from his hair. He felt as if he'd slept for days. (And he had, as he was about to find out.) He looked about him. He was standing on some sort of wooden platform with simple mattresses arranged in a row along it. Then he saw the top of a wooden ladder and climbed down it.

So this was Nyth Brân. One open room with a fireplace at one end and the raised wooden platform or 'croglofft' at the other, which was obviously some sort of bedroom for the whole family. Although it was morning, the place was still dark as there was just one, small window in the whole house. But Gethin could see well enough through the dim light to realise how poor and primitive everything was.

The door was open and a little weak November light came through that too, with a strong gust of wind on its tail. Gethin shivered and rubbed his eyes. When he opened them again, he saw Guto standing in the doorway.

"Come, breakfast," he said, leading Gethin to a low table with stools around it. The little girls were still staring at him. There was a woman by the fire – she had to be Guto's mam. She turned and smiled at him.

"Mam?" Gethin heard himself say, unable to believe his eyes. If the girls were the spitting image of each other, then this woman was the spitting image of Gethin's mam.

"You can call me Mam if that pleases you," said the smiling woman, adding, "Here are Marged and Mari, the twins. You met with Guto already."

Gethin smiled back at her, a little awkwardly. Then he heard a deep voice behind him.

"You can call me Tad, what's more."

Dad. Gethin turned. Here was the man who'd carried him through the wind and rain, all the way up to the holy spring. Gethin hadn't been able to see him properly through the driving rain and darkness. He stared at him now, open-mouthed. Before him stood a strong man, fit as a fiddle, with a pleasant face and a thick mop of hair that was starting to turn grey – exactly as Gethin had imagined his own dad!

"And your own name?" asked the man, smiling.

Gethin couldn't take his eyes off him. He gave himself a shake. He'd better answer, or he'd look rude.

"Gethin. Gethin Tanner."

"Tanner?" Gethin's surname meant nothing to him, as he didn't speak a word of English.

"Um, Tan . . . y . . . graig," said Gethin in a flash, trying to help him. Tan-y-graig meant 'beneath the rock' – and it sounded like a place name.

Guto's dad smiled. Now *this* was a name that made sense to him.

"I never heard tell of Tan-y-graig. Where be it?"

He obviously thought Tan-y-graig was the name of Gethin's home. Gethin tried to think of somewhere – anywhere – that was far enough away and that would have existed in this time. Then he remembered going for lunch in a pub in a little village near the town of Aberhonddu – or Brecon – with his mam and Gransha, some time ago when he was younger.

"It's in Llanfrynach," answered Gethin, hoping he'd chosen wisely.

"Llanfrynach . . ." said Guto's father, as if this was the first time he'd heard the name.

"Near Aberhonddu," Gethin added.

"You came from afar," said the older man in surprise, as if Aberhonddu was the other side of the world. Then he went on, "Guto tells us you've a-lost your parents and that you be destitute. Be of good cheer. This is your home now."

Gethin didn't know what to say, but it was obvious from the way Guto was shaking his head behind his father's back that he shouldn't tell the truth. So Gethin said the only thing he could: "Thank you."

And with that, the family sat down to breakfast – some sort of thin porridge – and Gethin was given the first turn at using the only available spoon.

~

"The Parish of Llanwynno is like to someone's head, that's been a-severed off," explained Guto, using a nail to carve a map on a large, smooth stone. Guto had shown Gethin around the farm after breakfast, and by now they were back in the farmyard. Now Guto wanted to make sure that Gethin got to know the rest of the parish, too. He continued: "The river Rhondda be the neck that's been a-torn in half . . ."

A torn-in-half neck? Gethin thought this sounded a bit gory, but he kept quiet. He didn't want to offend Guto.

". . . then we follow the river Taf towards the north, thus to make the jaw, the mouth and the nose – see you here?"

"I think so," answered Gethin, uncertainly.

"When once I've finished, you'll see better," said Guto, still making marks with his nail. "The river Cynon be the eyebrows and the forehead . . . and here be the crown – the woods of Coed Cae Aberaman . . . then the Rhondda Fach and the slopes of Cefn Gwyngul maketh the back of the head, which goes back down to the neck, where first we began."

"In other words, at the river Rhondda?"

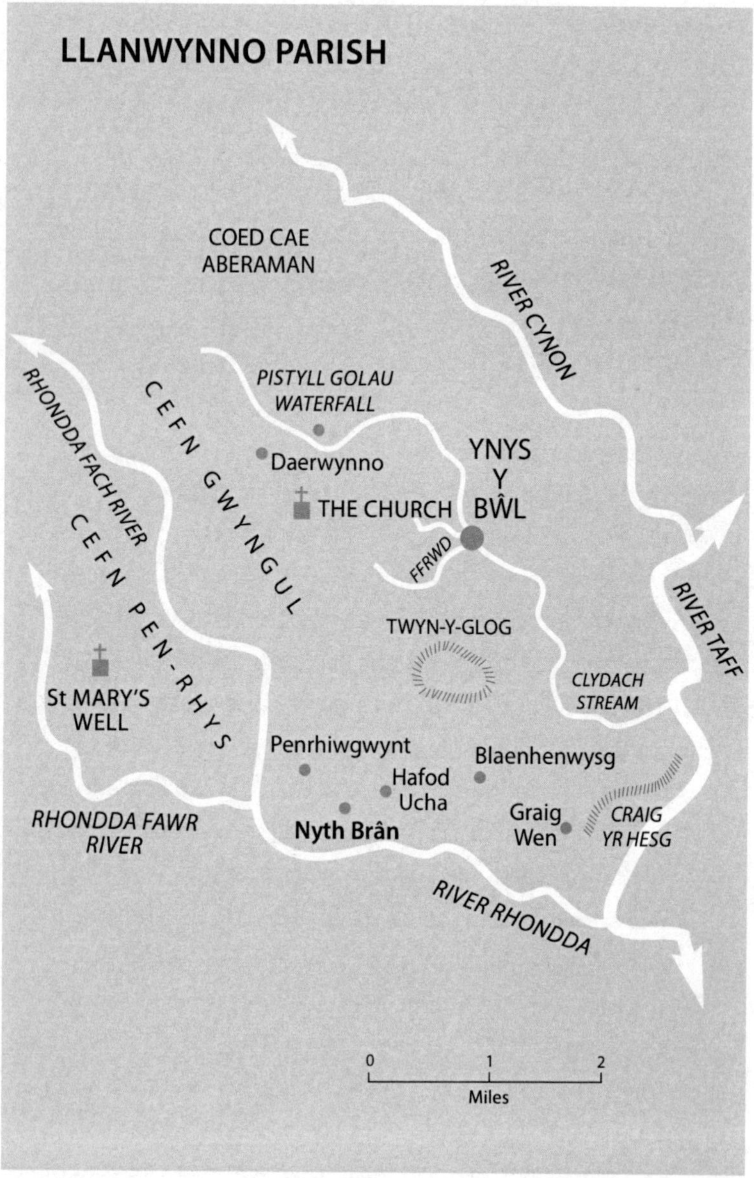

LLANWYNNO PARISH

COED CAE ABERAMAN

RIVER CYNON

RHONDDA FACH RIVER

CEFN GWYNGUL

PISTYLL GOLAU WATERFALL

Daerwynno

THE CHURCH

YNYS Y BŴL

FFRWD

CEFN PEN-RHYS

TWYN-Y-GLOG

RIVER TAFF

St MARY'S WELL

CLYDACH STREAM

Penrhiwgwynt

Blaenhenwysg

Hafod Ucha

Nyth Brân

Graig Wen

CRAIG YR HESG

RHONDDA FAWR RIVER

RIVER RHONDDA

0 1 2

Miles

"Just so," confirmed Guto, jabbing his nail to create spot after spot where the back of the head met the neck.

"And here be Nyth Brân. And there Hafod Ucha, Siencyn's home."

"Really close by," noted Gethin.

A little further down the neck, towards the jawline, was Blaenhenwysg, where Ifan lived. And a little further up the back of the head was Penrhiwgwynt, which was Dafydd's home. The parish church was right at the top of the head. Then Guto showed him other places that might interest him, before ending up in a very important spot.

". . . and to finish, here be Craig-yr-hesg," he said, pointing to a mark on the jaw. Gethin stared at it. So here was where he'd awoken, in the wood behind the rocks.

"Keep this about you safely, until you know the place better," said Guto, handing the stone to Gethin.

There was no chance to thank him because the Tri Trist – Dafydd, Ifan and Siencyn – arrived in the farmyard at exactly that moment. And they didn't look happy.

"What befell you? We were supposed to meet this morning!" complained Dafydd.

"Gethin awoke," explained Guto.

The boys stared at Gethin, wordlessly. It was obvious they felt unsure about him.

"It be not too late," suggested Guto.

"To do what?" asked Gethin.

"To hunt the Boncyn Wyla, that be what," answered Siencyn.

Gethin stared at him. What was he on about?

"To search for the Cyff Dolig," explained Ifan. But Gethin still didn't understand.

"I thought the tylwyth teg knew all there be to know," said Dafydd, peeved, when he saw the confusion on Gethin's face.

"Wisht, you rattlehead! What if my parents a-hear you?" hissed Guto, before turning to Gethin and explaining: "The Cyff Dolig, or the Christmas log, be a big piece of wood that we'll be a-laying on the fire come Christmas time. And the very biggest of all the Christmas logs be the Boncyn Wyla – and everyone will a-gather at the hearth of whoever has the good fortune to find it."

"Sort of competition, is it?" asked Gethin.

"There you are," said Guto, before turning back to the boys. "See? If you explain things a-simply and a-clearly to him, he understands right well."

Without further delay, the boys headed off for the big wood that covered the slope behind Nyth Brân. Gethin was glad for the chance to warm his legs up. It'd been cold, chatting in the farmyard with Guto. His feet were the worst, because he went barefoot now, like the rest. He winced as his big toe hit a stone, wondering how on earth he was going to cope, but the others didn't seem to be bothered at all. *They've probably walked barefoot all their lives*, he thought. One thing was for sure – his mam would have a pink fit if she saw him now, especially as they were roving about on their own, without adults.

When they reached the edge of the wood the other boys fell silent.

"Is something wrong?" asked Gethin.

"Er – no. Nothing wrong," denied Siencyn, pulling his hand through his thick red hair. But Gethin could see from his worried expression that this wasn't true.

"They be afraid of the bwci-bo," Guto laughed.

This time Gethin understood the word. The bwci-bo was a ghost.

"Not the bwci-bo," protested Ifan. "Rhys caught a glimpse of the Hen Ŵr y Coed here, a bit ago." The Hen Ŵr y Coed – the Old Man of the Woods.

"Rhys be Ifan's older brother," Guto explained to Gethin.

"Be that as it may, the Hen Ŵr y Coed wanders the woods hereabouts . . ." continued Ifan.

"A-searching for childer to catch and to eat!" Dafydd interrupted, his eyes wide with alarm.

"Stuff and nonsense! He's but a poor old feller with no home to go to – that be all. Dad a-told me that," said Guto.

"But he be not half as frightful as Cadwcan y Fwyall," added Dafydd, ignoring Guto.

"Now *that* one would tear you into pieces, like to this," agreed Siencyn, pulling a fearsome face and miming Cadwgan's vicious actions with his hands. "And then he a-spears the meat on branches, for the crows to feast upon."

Even Siencyn had turned pale at this point, and Dafydd and Ifan didn't look much better.

"You lot of lily-livers!" pooh-poohed Guto. "I be not a-feared – not of anything."

At that very moment something flapped up before them – a startling flash of blue, brown and white – unleashing a wild scream of alarm. Everyone – including Guto – jumped out of their skins. Then the boys ducked to hide in the undergrowth, before getting up again like a bunch of fools when they realised that it was just a bird. The only one who hadn't moved was Gethin, because he'd frozen in fear. But, to the others, Gethin had looked brave and fearless.

"Were you not a-feared?" asked Dafydd in awe.

"Of course he weren't a-feared," Guto answered for him. "What would a-frighten Gethin, him being a . . . well, you know."

Guto was avoiding the words 'tylwyth teg' on purpose – it was unlucky to mention them too often. Gethin didn't say anything. He was trying to act confident but he was still shaking, especially as he couldn't help feeling that someone really was watching them.

"You be not about to leave us here alone, be you, and vanish back to the other world?" Ifan asked him, fearfully.

Gethin shook his head and saw the relief flood poor Ifan's face.

Then they ventured deeper into the damp darkness of the woods. Gethin kept close to Guto, until Guto saw something in the distance, gave a start then rushed away, shouting "There be a good one!"

When the others caught him up, they had to agree. The log at their feet was the ideal size to fill the hearth at Nyth Brân. Not too long, yet really thick. The only problem was – how on earth were they going to shift it?

"Perchance Gethin will put an enchantment on the log," said Ifan.

"Good idea!" agreed Siencyn. They all turned to him, expectantly.

Gethin tried to think quickly. "I . . . er, I'm really sorry to disappoint you, but my powers don't work so well in this world."

He watched as four faces fell.

"*We'll* never be able to carry it, that be for sure," grumbled Siencyn.

"But we could try rolling it," suggested Gethin.

And that's what they did, with Guto praising Gethin's clever idea all the way, and the others complaining that it was still pretty hard work. Gethin knew the 'Tri Trist' hadn't warmed to him yet. He sighed to himself, thinking, sadly, that he was used to people not warming to him. But he took great comfort from the thought that Guto, at least, seemed to like him.

11

The rain had stopped by the time the whole family – including Gethin – set out for the parish church, Eglwys Wynno. But the wind was just as fierce, so they all strode quickly through the wood behind the farm to try to keep warm, wrapping their wool cloaks tightly about them. After climbing and climbing they left the wood behind them and the ground began to level off. Then, before him, Gethin saw a small hill that rose from the flat ground in a neat and tidy bump.

"What be the name of that hillock?" asked Guto, testing him.

Gethin scratched his head. It was on the tip of his tongue! Then it came to him in a flash. "Twyn-y-glog," he answered.

Guto laughed and clapped him on the back, delighted with his pupil. In no time they'd reached the foot of Twyn-y-glog and joined another, wider, path. Then the twins, little Marged and Mari, began to moan that their legs were tired, even though their parents told them they were nearly there. To take their minds off things, Guto challenged them to a race and Gethin joined in. Even hopping on one leg, Guto streaked far ahead of the rest. But when he saw the twins were tiring, he slowed to let them win.

Now Gethin could see other people, strangers, in the distance. But although Guto and the twins ran ahead to greet them, Gethin waited for his foster parents to catch him up. This was the first time Gethin had been out in public with the Nyth Brân family, and he felt nervous and shy. Most of all, he didn't want to let them down by doing anything wrong.

It was Gŵyl Domas – St Thomas's Day – a special day where all the people who lived in the parish came to church, even though it was only a few days till Christmas. This was the day to remember St Thomas the Apostle and those in need – for, after the service, a gift of money was shared amongst the ten poorest people in the parish.

Gethin was surprised when the church came into view. The building was so simple and basic that it looked more like a barn than a holy building. He was also surprised by the large crowd of children and young people crowding together by the church gate, shouting and laughing like unruly schoolkids before the first bell. But there was a big difference: every single one of them was speaking Welsh, not English. Gethin saw Guto's friends – Ifan, Dafydd and Siencyn – but there was no time to join them because the service was about to start.

As the family sat down on one of the wooden benches at the back, people turned in their seats to stare at Gethin, trying to guess who this young stranger was. Guto's mam squeezed his hand, aware of his nerves. She'd explained to him before they'd set off that everyone in the parish knew everyone else, so they were going to tell people that Gethin was Guto's cousin. That way, Gethin wouldn't have to be sent back to his own parish after a certain amount of time, which was the law.

They wanted to keep Gethin with them, to treat him as a second son. For, ever since Gethin had been cured by the holy water of Ffynnon Fair, his new parents had believed he was a present from the Virgin Mary. Gethin squeezed her hand back, and smiled up at her. He felt very lucky to be part of the Nyth Brân family.

To avoid the staring eyes, Gethin looked down at the earth floor and nudged the straw strewn across it with his bare feet. The church looked pretty similar to a barn inside too. Then he heard the priest's voice, from up the front. The service was about to begin and Gethin relaxed, knowing that from now on everyone's attention would be on the priest – not on him.

After the service, all the young people rushed outside, Gethin amongst them, while the grown-ups followed more sedately, greeting one another, sharing stories and laughter, enjoying the chance to catch up with parish news and gossip.

Guto and the other kids were chucking a ball about, right in front of the church. It was some sort of game, like a cross between football and rugby, but Gethin couldn't work out the rules – if there *were* any. Then Guto yelled, throwing the ball at him. Gethin caught it, before running straight into someone – oof! – and losing it again. He felt a real fool, especially when he caught a glimpse of Dafydd and Siencyn through the crowd, shaking their heads scornfully at his clumsiness. As he turned to give the kid he'd knocked over a hand up, he froze. It was Nathan! Or, rather, someone just like him, but different at the same time, because the boy lying on the ground, groaning, wasn't a big, strong, strapping lad. He was thin, pale and weak-looking.

"Nathaniel!" shouted someone. "Get up, you milk-sop! Stand and fight!"

Gethin saw a tall, furious-looking man shoving through the crowd. He was yelling at the boy to get up and defend himself, this time in broken English. But Nathaniel stayed curled on the ground, putting up his arms to protect his head. Gethin saw, to his horror, that the man had a whip in his hand, the sort that jockeys use. He lifted it and brought it down on the boy, mercilessly, again and again, turning back to Welsh.

"Get up! Get up! You useless, lily-livered wastrel!"

Gethin had frozen in place. But Guto hadn't. In a flash,

he'd leapt over Nathaniel, placing himself between the boy and his father. The man raised his whip again and Gethin felt his stomach shrink. But before he had the chance to bring it down on Guto, Guto's dad strode up from behind and snatched the weapon from his grip.

"Enough is enough," said Guto's father, calmly and firmly.

The man stared at him for a moment with narrowed eyes before hauling his son to his feet and dragging him away, pushing the other children aside. Then Guto's dad took the ball from Gethin's hands and threw it into the air – a sign for the game to continue.

The other kids shouted and jumped for the ball, but Gethin stood aside. He was shaken to the core. Not just because of what he'd seen, but because something very strange was happening to him . . .

The similarity between Guto's mam and his own . . . Guto's dad was exactly like Gethin had imagined his own dad . . . Guto's best friends were the spitting image of the Tri Trist . . . And poor Nathaniel, though so cowed and frightened, was just like Nathan. Gethin stared at the other children's faces. He could have sworn that lots of them were familiar – kids he'd seen in the schoolyard. But though he looked for her everywhere, there was no sign of anyone like Caitlin.

Worse luck.

12

The basket was full of delicious things: apples, biscuits, a whole, round cheese, bara brith – a kind of fruit loaf – and even a piece of salted ham.

"Your turn," said Guto, passing the basket to Siencyn.

"Oof. Pretty heavy," sighed Siencyn, gripping it tightly. It was the first day of 1714 and the boys were going from farm to farm and cottage to cottage, collecting calennig – that is, good things to eat in exchange for a special, new year's song.

"Do you gather calennig in the other world?" Ifan asked Gethin.

Gethin thought about it. "We do, except we get sweets as presents. We do it at Hallowe'en," he answered.

"Of course. All Hallow's Eve. The night of the dead, when spirits be free to roam where they will . . ." said Dafydd, shivering. He eyed Gethin suspiciously.

"Ma-a-ny a fearful wraith will wander the country on that night. Phantasms like to the Hwch Ddu Gwta, the tail-less black sow – a very monster, that is wont to eat childer who be foolish enough to venture out late," intoned Dafydd.

"Were you out a-hunting calennig when once you lost your way and came out in Craig-yr-hesg?" asked Siencyn, slyly.

"An end to this foolish questioning!" ordered Guto, noticing Gethin's discomfort, and the five of them tramped on in silence.

Despite the warm welcome at Nyth Brân, Gethin knew that Guto's best friends still hadn't completely accepted him.

Even during the Christmas festivities – as they'd walked to church first thing on Christmas day, carrying candles; or in all the merriment of celebrating the Boncyn Wyla at Nyth Brân, when the home-brewed beer and laughter had flowed freely and everyone had enjoyed sweet, flat-bread cakes in front of the roaring fire – Gethin had felt them keeping their distance.

And it wasn't just the Tri Trist that were unsure of him. Gethin had felt other children's eyes, staring at him at the plygain service on Christmas morning, as members of the parish stood to sing holy songs in harmonies. (And, though he'd looked and looked, there still was no sign of Caitlin amongst them.) He'd tried to push the uncomfortable feelings away and concentrate instead on how beautiful the church looked, with tens and tens of candles lighting the place in the early-morning, winter darkness. It had been like floating in the middle of the Milky Way.

Or being at the Hallowe'en party in Caitlin's house, thought Gethin now. *Or looking down on the lights of Pontypridd from the top of Graig Wen.* Gethin felt the most terrible pang of hiraeth – homesickness, sadness and longing.

"Call we next at the house of Richard Edwards?" suggested Guto, interrupting Gethin's thoughts. But the feeling of hiraeth was still very strong so, to try to sound brave and cheerful, he said, "Why not?"

"Because that man's the very devil, that's why not!" protested Ifan.

"Gethin is like to our lucky talisman, mark you. Even the devil himself couldn't hurt a hair of the head of one of the tylwyth teg," said Guto.

"Unless the member of the tylwyth teg has a-left all his magic in the other world," complained Dafydd.

"Know you that Gethin has more magical powers than you shall ever even dream of, Dafydd Penrhiwgwynt!" snapped Guto.

Then Siencyn began to giggle. Dafydd glared at him indignantly, before turning to Gethin.

"Very well. So long as it be you who knocks at the door and sings," he said. "Perchance you have enough magical talent for that?"

"Yes," answered Gethin, as sure as he could manage, "course I have." But he was regretting opening his mouth already. Richard Edwards was the nasty piece of work who'd beaten his son, Nathaniel, outside the church, some ten days ago . . .

Guto had filled him in after that. According to him, Richard Edwards thought he was better than everyone in the parish because he managed three farms that belonged to a rich family who lived elsewhere. He lived in a grand house – far too grand, in Guto's opinion – and employed loads of servants and maids. But maybe the most important thing – from Guto's point of view – was that his mam had refused to marry him and had chosen Guto's dad instead. Now things were so bad between the two men that no one could even speak the name of Richard Edwards at Nyth Brân.

All this was whirling about in Gethin's head as the gang wound their way towards Plas Coch, the home of Richard Edwards – or Dic Coed Coch (Dick Red Trees) as everyone called him behind his back. Richard Edwards hated the nickname – it sounded far too Welsh for his liking and he had pretensions to being a civilised gentleman, who spoke English.

Plas Coch came into view. Gethin hadn't seen a building like it since arriving here. It was a two-storey, rectangular stone house, with nine glass windows at the front alone. To the side, there were cowsheds and a large barn, and something strange, the shape of an upside-down ice-cream cone, made of stone.

"See you that stone hut by there?" asked Guto. "It be a pig sty. They say that Nathaniel is made to sleep there, oftentimes, after his father has a-given him a beating."

"And we be not talking a little cuff on the ear. We be talking a walloping and a half," added Ifan.

Gethin shivered – he could easily imagine it. By now the last thing he wanted to do was knock on Richard Edwards's door. But it was too late to back out now, as they were walking through the open gate and heading around the building to the back door. The others kept their distance as Gethin stepped up to the doorstep. He counted to three and knocked. Then he waited. No one came. He looked around, relieved, but the rest were gesturing for him to try again. So he knocked once more.

The door opened and Gethin almost fell backwards in shock. Before him stood a short, muscular man with a scarred, creased face. But however wrinkled his skin, he was the spitting image of someone Gethin knew: Cai Thomas! And he was staring at Gethin with dark, narrowed eyes.

"So? What have you to say? Or do you merely stand and stare, like to a dumb statue?" asked the man.

Gethin cleared his throat and began to sing: "Calennig wyf yn mofyn, Ddydd Calan ddechreu'r flwyddyn . . . For calennig I'm a-asking, On New Year's Day, The start of the year . . ."

But he'd only sung the first two lines before the scarred man raised his hand and snapped, "Stop your noise, sirrah – that be enough! Stay where you are. I'll give you calennig, all right." Then he disappeared before coming back with a bulging sackcloth bag.

"Careful now. There be eggs in that bag, and other sweetmeats besides," he said, handing it over.

"Thank you very much. And a happy new year to you," said Gethin.

"Happy new year to you too, my good sire," the man answered, bowing and smirking. Gethin was glad when he went back inside and slammed the door.

"Who on earth was he?" Gethin asked, walking over to the others.

"That be Ianto. Richard Edwards's most faithful servant," answered Siencyn. "And a man with many a twist in his tail."

"He'd sell his own mother for a penny," agreed Ifan.

"Put you the things in the basket and we'll go," said Dafydd impatiently, eager to get out of there. Gethin reached into the bag and pulled out a handful of eggs. But in his haste he let one slip from his hands to smash to the ground.

"Look you at what you've done!" said Dafydd, before gagging and clutching at his nose. The stench hit Gethin next and he almost vomited. It'd been a rotten egg. Then they heard a cackling sound. Through the little window by the back door they saw Ianto, his scarred face cracking up with laughter.

"You pig!" shouted Guto, hurling one of the eggs at the window. Splotch. Dripping egg yolk snaked slowly down the window-glass. As they all grabbed an egg each, Ianto came rushing out of the house like a goblin, waving a thick staff.

"Want a taste of this, do you, you mongrel curs, you!"

Guto hurled another egg at him. It missed, landing behind Ianto as he strode across the farmyard towards them. Dafydd missed too. So did Siencyn. And Ifan. All the boys were backing off at speed, still facing Ianto. All the boys, except Gethin. He'd frozen in fear . . . and Ianto was fast closing in on him.

"Gethin! Move!" shouted Guto.

Before he knew what he was doing, Gethin took aim and threw the egg in his hand. It went arcing through the air and hit Ianto right in the middle of his forehead. Ianto stood stock still, as if he'd been shot, as the egg's contents slithered down his face. Then he unleashed a scream as the stink hit his nostrils and he fell to his knees, gagging convulsively.

"Quick!" shouted Guto, grabbing Gethin's arm and pulling on it.

"Loose the hounds! Loose the hounds!" shouted Ianto hoarsely to the servants who'd come pouring out of the house to see what was going on. The hunting hounds of Plas Coch were famous throughout the land for their speed – and their ferocity.

"Run for your lives, boys!" shouted Guto. He didn't need to tell them twice. In a wink, five pairs of legs were pumping hell for leather towards the iron gate at the entrance. Gethin was last, but in no time he'd sprinted through the gates, passing Siencyn. Then Ifan. Then even Dafydd, who was the fastest of them all – apart from Guto, of course.

He ran. And ran. And ran.

"Don't leave us behind, Gethin!" shouted Siencyn after him, his voice weak with exertion. Only then did Gethin realise how far ahead of the other three he was. He began to slow down, as if his brain was squeezing the brakes.

Then he stood, hands on hips and catching his breath, as Guto came jogging back to him.

"We be safe now," he said, hardly even out of breath. The others arrived one by one, panting and wheezing. There was no sign of the hunting dogs. Perhaps they'd eaten too much over the Christmas holidays and were busy sleeping it off.

"Saw you ever such a thing? David couldn't have hit Goliath better!" laughed Siencyn.

"Right in the middle of his ugly face, it was!" said Ifan.

"Saw you how fast our Gethin runs? Like the wind, he was!" said Dafydd. There was admiration in his voice.

"See you? He hasn't lost all his magical powers – o ye of little faith," boasted Guto proudly, slinging an arm round Gethin's shoulders.

Gethin smiled to himself. If they believed he had magical powers, so much the better. He wasn't sure exactly how he'd been able to aim so well, or to run so fast. But he didn't really care. The most important thing was that he'd impressed the others. And as they clapped him on the back and laughed, he realised that he had three new friends, at last.

13

"Ma hoo! Ma hoo!" bawled Guto, driving Gethin, Ifan, Dafydd and Siencyn before him – just like the ploughman had driven his oxen when he'd come to plough their fields for sowing spring oats.

Gethin had taken it for granted that horses would pull the plough (after all, he knew it wouldn't be a tractor!) so he'd been surprised to see two bull-like animals turning up about two weeks ago, with the ploughman. Even better, gripping the plough's wooden handles to steady the blade as it sliced deep into the earth while the oxen sweated and pulled before him, the ploughman had begun to sing:

"Dou ych yw Sicl a Sowin,
un coch a'r nall yn felyn.
Pan yn aretig yn eu chwys
Nhw dorran gŵys i'r blewyn."

"Two fine ox be Sicl and Sowin
One be red and the other be brown
When they sweat to pull the plough
Deep cuts the blade into the ground."

He was singing praises to his oxen, saying how great they were at their work. But this turned out to be just the first of many songs, because he kept it up the whole time he ploughed – for hours and hours – while the boys followed him every step of the way, singing along raucously.

"Ma hoo! Ma hoo!" shouted Guto again, shooing the boys in front of him even faster.

The gang was in a great mood. The spring sun was shining down and they were heading for all the fun of the fair – on their way to the fair at Ynys-y-bŵl, one of the most important events in the parish calendar. This fair marked a turning point in the year – summer was on the horizon, and the cold, wintry days of January and February, when everyone had holed up at home, feeding their animals and fixing farm tools, felt far behind them now. During those long, dark winter evenings, people had gathered in neighbours' homes, making rush candles or weaving and knitting by firelight. And whenever people were gathered about a warm hearth, someone would tell a story.

When it came to Gethin's turn, he'd chosen a bit from *The Hobbit*, pretending it was an old tale from his birthplace near Aberhonddu. But Guto had believed it to be a real story from the land of the tylwyth teg, and he'd listened, spellbound, to every word. Gethin had felt a bit bad about this. Sometimes he was tempted to tell Guto the truth – that he came from the future, not the other world – but in the end he always decided not to. It would be too hard to explain. And Guto might feel hurt that Gethin hadn't told him the truth straight off.

Back on the road to Ynys-y-bŵl, Guto began another of the ploughman's songs. The others joined in, belting out the words, over and over:

"Mi fuo lawar blwyddyn
yn canu gyta'r ychin,

bara haidd a chosyn cnap,
dim tishan lap na phwtin – ma hw!"
"For many, many a year and ten
I been a-singing with my oxen
Give me oat bread and a lump of cheese
No puddin' or plate cake for me – ma hoo!"

In the end they had to stop singing because their voices were hoarse and they were all laughing too much. And by that time they'd almost reached Ynys-y-bŵl.

They could hear the hurly-burly of the fair long before the village came into view, and such a great hub-bub of sound rose from the place that Gethin was surprised to see that Ynys-y-bŵl was just a few dozen cottages clustered together. And to think this was the biggest settlement in the parish! But as they crossed the bridge over the Clydach brook he was even more surprised to see the huge crowds of people who'd flocked to the fair.

There were hundreds there, many more than lived in the parish itself, and there were even more things up for sale: animals, farm produce and goods of all sorts. And the sound, after the quiet of winter, was deafening – the crowds were gossiping, joking, laughing, arguing and bargaining keenly as they bought and sold, while the animals bleated and roared. A handful of ballad-singers were doing their best to make their voices heard above the din, singing the latest penillion – poetry set to music – and trying to sell pamphlets of the songs' words at the same time. There was even a fool-hardy crew of actors, performing an interlude – a kind of comic drama – on top of a cart, while the audience shouted over them to one another.

Soon the boys were amongst it all and suddenly they too had to shout to be heard.

Guto grabbed Gethin's arm and pointed out a gang of youths, older boys from their own parish, who were strutting cockily about the place. Later, predicted Guto, after the beer had flowed, there'd be a fight between this gang and the big boys from the other parishes. But the rivalry between the parishes was nothing compared to that between the 'blaenau' and the 'bro'. Blaenau Morgannwg was the high ground from Llantrisant to Merthyr, and Bro Morgannwg was the lowlands from Pen-y-Bont to Caerdydd, down towards the sea. When these two got together – look out!

"We be Blaenau boys, remember you that," said Guto, deadly serious.

Gethin began to feel uneasy – were there any Bro boys here today? – until Guto confirmed that they'd have left the fair and started back for Nyth Brân long before things began hotting up.

Then Gethin felt something tugging at his leg. He looked down, and to his astonishment saw a nanny goat chewing happily on his trousers. Gethin tried to gently push it away but the animal was as stubborn as anything, so in the end he gave her a little kick to try to dislodge her. The next thing he knew, something sprang at him from behind and knocked him to the ground before laying into him with small, strong fists. In shock, Gethin did his best to shield his face and defend himself while Guto – with Ifan, Dafydd and Siencyn's help – managed to drag whoever it was off him.

He got up, shakily, and turned to see a wild-looking girl

glaring at him. His heart leapt. Because, although it was red with fury and topped with a haystack of untidy black hair, he knew that face: Caitlin! Or, at least, a smaller version of her. She wasn't much bigger than Gethin, if at all, but despite her size she was obviously a dangerous little mite.

"Let Mabli alone, you bwbach!" she spat.

"I'm sorry," said Gethin. He couldn't take his eyes off her, torn between joy at seeing 'Caitlin' at last and fear of this furious girl.

"What be the matter? Never seed a girl before?"

"Never seed a one that's like to you, that's for sure," answered Guto on Gethin's behalf. At this, the girl began to struggle even more, so Guto and the others were forced to let go their grip on her. With a scornful glance in Gethin's direction, she turned on her heel and dragged Mabli and another, unnamed, goat away.

"Who was *that*?" asked Gethin, once he'd found his voice.

"Catrin – or Catws, as everyone calls her," answered Guto, adding, "Best you keep away from her. She be a wild one. Temper like the very devil on her. And a real sachabwndi." Seeing that Gethin didn't understand, he went on, "Ragamuffin. Scarecrow. Looks like to a tramp."

"What's more, her family be quakers," added Dafydd.

"Quakers?" asked Gethin.

"You know. Nonconformists," explained Dafydd.

But Gethin was still none the wiser.

"Heathens," said Guto. "People who don't go to church, and worship instead in houses, or some common barn."

Gethin was about to say that Llanwynno Church wasn't

much more than a barn, but he managed to stop himself in time.

"And they shake like this," said Siencyn, shivering madly whilst his eyes bulged open wide. The rest doubled up in laughter.

Then, "Siencyn Hafod Ucha. As foolish as ever, I see."

It was the voice of a man, from behind them. They spun to see Richard Edwards, Nathaniel's father. Behind him was Nathaniel himself, staring at the ground.

"I have heard tell of you, Gethin of Llanfrynach," said Richard Edwards, studying him with narrowed eyes.

Gethin wasn't sure how to respond, so he put out his hand. The man smirked. "Bit of a *gentleman*, I see," he sneered, using the English word.

Then he made a big show of shaking Gethin's hand, before dropping it and saying in English, "*Talking to fools why I be?*"

Gethin frowned. Then, without thinking, he corrected him: "*You mean, Why am I talking to idiots?*"

Richard Edwards's eyes narrowed even further. "So. Speaks the *gentleman* English!"

"Yes, he does. And a deal better than you do, what's more!" said Guto.

At this, the man frowned furiously and stalked off, followed obediently by Nathaniel. The boy hadn't once raised his eyes from the ground.

"Can you really speak English?" asked Ifan. He sounded stunned.

"Course he can, you rattlehead! Heard you him!" laughed Dafydd.

"Can you read and write, to boot?" ventured Siencyn.

"Yes, I can," answered Gethin. "But it's not a big deal. Where I come from, almost everyone can."

The boys stared at him in admiration, shook their heads in amazement then grabbed his arms and dragged him, laughing, into the midst of the merry crowd. And from then on, as they wandered about and enjoyed the fun of the fair, the boys pestered Gethin to teach them a word or two of English – swear words, mostly – and laughed their heads off at how funny the strange words sounded.

Though he was having a great time with his friends, Gethin couldn't help keeping half an eye out for Catws, with her wild black hair to match her temper and her two pet goats. But there was no sign of her anywhere.

14

The sky was completely blue, apart from one, white cloud, floating high above like a long, thin finger pointing to something far, far away. In the bright sunshine, the hills around Nyth Brân and the meadows below formed a brilliant, green patchwork. *The world's so beautiful sometimes*, thought Gethin. And this world was especially beautiful. It was as if he was seeing the whole place in colour for the very first time, after everything being in black and white. By now he'd learned the names of all the trees, plants, birds and animals that surrounded him. He knew now that the screaming bird they'd met when they'd hunted for the Boncyn Wyla was a 'sgrech-y-coed', or jay, and that the 'hesg' in the name Craig-yr-hesg was a tall plant with strong stems and thick leaves – bulrushes.

Smiling to himself, Gethin got back to the task in hand – searching for one of Nyth Brân's sheep, that had gone astray. Gethin and Guto had been shepherding on the hills far above the farm and had spent the night in one of the little stone shepherds' huts, or bothies, that dotted the hilltops.

Bothies were simple but snug buildings – and sleeping in them was definitely more comfortable than being out under the stars, because the nights were still pretty cold, though the days were getting warmer.

Though they'd searched the slopes all morning, the lost sheep was nowhere to be found. So Guto suggested they head for the marshes beyond the church, warning Gethin to take care, because the ground there was full of deep, dangerous sinkholes. Many animals had disappeared into the bog. And so had one or two unlucky people. Gethin really didn't fancy venturing out on to the marsh, but he didn't want to show Guto he was scared so he agreed.

If the slopes of the hills had shone in the sun, it was as if the marsh sucked in the sunshine and swallowed it, because all Gethin could see before him when they got there was acres of colourless, menacing-looking ground.

Suddenly, they heard a cry – the cry of something in trouble. Guto rushed towards the sound and Gethin sprinted after him. It wasn't easy to keep up with Guto, but the last thing Gethin wanted was to be left in the middle of this vast, dangerous bog on his own.

The cries grew louder as they approached. It was a goat, stuck fast in one of the marsh's treacherous holes and bleating for her life. And who should be staring at her in panic, not knowing what to do, but Catws. Gethin's heart leapt. When Catws saw the boys, her eyes grew even wider and she took a step back, as if expecting them to attack her. Gethin raised his hand and said, without thinking, "Don't worry. We'll help you."

Gethin wasn't sure who was more surprised to hear this, Guto or Catws. If he'd had a mirror, he'd have seen his own surprise, too. Why on earth had he offered to help? What could he do?

But before he knew what he was doing, Gethin fell to his knees on the wet ground and shouted to Guto to hold tight to his heels. Then he dragged himself across the perilously soft peat towards the goat, like a soldier crawling on his stomach.

The goat was up to her haunches in the hole and her large brown eyes gaped wide, full of fear, while she bleating hoarsely. The ground here was like a sponge and Gethin could feel himself sinking into it but, by managing not to panic and keeping his body totally flat, he was able to reach out and grab the goat by her horns. She looked wretched and bedraggled and she stank to high heavens, like mouldy old cheese or football socks that'd been stuffed into a games bag and forgotten. Gethin did his best to ignore the smell as he gripped the animal tightly and yelled "Pull, Guto!" But though Guto yanked on his heels with all his might and

Gethin's ankles felt like they were going to snap, Gethin didn't move one centimetre. Nor did the goat.

"You too, Catws!" shouted Gethin.

Catws grabbed his right heel while Guto pulled on the left one, the two of them groaning with effort. Gethin gripped the goat even harder. His arms were hurting now almost as much as his ankles. He thought, *This is hopeless*, then, with a great sucking, shifting sound, the bog began to release the goat and he felt himself sliding back, very slowly, with the goat safe in his arms.

Once he was on more stable ground, Gethin released the goat. The poor animal was shaking all over and Catws leapt forward to hug her. "Wisht, my little Mabli, my little one," murmured Catws, over and over, as if she was singing a lullaby.

Guto grinned, turning to Gethin and whispering that the two nanny goats were as stinky and dishevelled as each other. Angrily, and without thinking, Gethin elbowed Guto in his side. The blow was harder than he'd intended, and tears of pain and shock sprang to Guto's eyes. Gethin felt bad at once, but before he had the chance to apologise, Catws was hugging him too – in spite of the fact that he was almost as muddy as the goat.

"Thank you," said Catws, shyly. Then she asked them if they'd like to come back to her home to have something to eat. Gethin agreed at once, though he could see that Guto wasn't keen at all.

~

No one said a word as they trekked across the marshy ground to Catws's house – even the goat had stopped bleating now and was following Catws obediently. Gethin could see that Guto was keeping his distance from Catws – he was obviously still suspicious of her. But Gethin felt the opposite. He wasn't nervous of Catws any more – he just wanted to be her friend. So he tried to catch her eye and smile at her. And, after a few unsuccessful attempts, he was rewarded with a tiny smile back.

After half an hour, they arrived at Catws's home. Two little children were out the front, chasing chickens and laughing happily.

"You naughty childer!" called Catws. She was only pretending to scold them, but they stopped their game at once, looking even more alarmed when they saw the two strange boys with her. Forgetting all about the chickens they ran into the house to hide.

Rhydygwreiddyn – Catws's house – was a bleak and sad-looking place. Nyth Brân, though so basic, was like a palace compared to this hovel, thought Gethin. Then he realised that the house was made of earth, just like the one in the original name for Pontypridd. Catws turned and beckoned for them to follow her inside.

"Better we don't," whispered Guto to Gethin, adding, "Perchance we won't come out alive."

"Don't be silly. Come on," said Gethin. He'd spoken loudly – too loudly – and he saw Catws's eyes fall as she realised something was wrong. But Guto wouldn't move. He shook his stubborn head and insisted on waiting in the yard outside.

Gethin turned to Catws. "Guto doesn't feel like eating." Then he followed Catws into the house, where he got another little smile from her, as a thank you for trying not to hurt her feelings. It was obvious that Catws knew very well why Guto didn't want to cross the threshold.

Inside, the hovel was even more miserable than outside and it was very dark in here, as if someone had pulled the curtains tightly closed to shut out the sun. In fact there was just one tiny, glassless window in the whole house. Gethin's nose itched from the smoky air that filled the room and a sour smell hit his nostrils – something like leather or the whiskey that Gransha drank sometimes. As his eyes grew used to the weak light and the smoke, he saw the two little children staring fearfully at him from the darkness under the croglofft and a woman bent over a small iron pot that hung above a smouldering peat fire.

"Mam – this be Gethin. The goat went a-wandering on the marsh. Gethin saved her."

"The blessings of the Lord be upon you, my boy," said Catws's mam, smiling kindly at him before turning her attention back to whatever was in the pot.

Then Catws handed him a piece of oat-cake and a wooden bowl full of some sort of liquid. "Goat's milk," she explained.

Gethin lifted the bowl to his lips. It smelled of old socks, just like the goat, but he didn't want to offend Catws so he swallowed the liquid quickly. It was surprisingly good – creamy and refreshing. He took another gulp and Catws laughed. Gethin realised he now had a milk-moustache, so he grinned and wiped his lips. Then, without warning, Catws planted a kiss on his check. Gethin felt himself blush and caught a tiny smile on Catws's mam's face at all this.

Catws laughed again, showing a row of perfect teeth, like pearls – that were especially beautiful because everything else about her was so raggle-taggle.

~

Catws's infectious laughter was still echoing in Gethin's head as he and Guto walked back to the bothy. They hadn't spoken a word since leaving Catws's house. From the corner of his eye, Gethin could see that Guto was looking at him, trying to catch his attention.

"What manner of a place was it, then?" asked Guto, at last.

"If you'd come inside, you'd know," answered Gethin shortly, adding, "What on earth were you expecting to see in there? The devil's head?"

With that, Gethin strode ahead and Guto trailed behind, head down. Then Gethin softened.

"If you'll accept Catws as a friend and not to make fun of her or her family for being different, I'll forgive you for being so mean about her."

"I won't. I do promise you," said Guto, shame in his voice.

The bothy came into view and there was the herd, grazing happily nearby. And, to their relief, the lost sheep was back in their midst.

That night, Guto told the funny story of how he'd once had to save not a goat but Ifan Blaenhenwysg, after he'd climbed too high up a tree and got stuck. Gethin smiled and laughed in all the right places. But he was only half listening, really. He was still revelling in today's events. He'd been brave enough to save the goat and had risked his own life in the process. The old Gethin would never have done that.

Never in a million years.

15

The old Gethin would never have rugby-tackled a sheep either, and dragged it into the pool near the Pistyll Golau waterfall to dip its fleece. Guto and the others were all there too – including Catws – helping the farmhands wash the sheep before shearing. The men were standing waist-deep in the river, gripping each sheep and swishing it back and forth through the water before passing it to other men on the bank who grabbed the animals tightly to squeeze as much water out of their fleeces as they could.

Suddenly, a sheep leapt from a man's arms and swam madly for shore. Without thinking, Gethin lunged into the water and dragged it back to him.

"There goes the Arwr y Gors!" the man shouted, taking an even firmer grip on the sheep. Arwr y Gors – Hero of the Marsh!

"He be master of the sheep's horn too – as well as the goat's!" shouted someone else. All the farmers and farmhands broke into laughter, and Gethin and his gang laughed with them. Everyone in the parish of Llanwynno – and beyond – had heard tell of Gethin's bravery by now, thanks to Guto.

And, as the story had spread, everyone that heard it had added some little detail of their own, like decoration. The goat became two goats, then three, and before long half a dozen – and Gethin, it was said, had swam through a slime-filled lake and battled swamp-monsters to save them then carried them back, three on each arm. Complete nonsense, of course, and no one really believed it all, but Gethin was happy when he heard these stories. It felt good to have a little attention for once. He'd had lots of praise from Guto's parents for saving the goat, too – and that had meant a lot. Because, although they were a little unsure about Catws's family's religion, they were agreed that 'the wench wasn't to blame for that'.

After the sheep had been washed, Dafydd was fool enough to call Catws a rattle-brained quaker, and had been thrown to the ground for his troubles. Catws, it turned out, was a master of 'ymaflyd codwm' – an old sporting contest that was like a mix between wrestling and judo. Her brother, Gwilym, had taught her before he'd died of measles when he was twelve. That was when Catws had stepped into his shoes as the family goatherd. Gwilym's strength – and temper – were legendary. But, if anything, the gang were more afraid of Catws than they'd ever been of him.

Now they laughed to see Dafydd groaning on the ground.

"Not a one of you could have done better, you dunderheads!" shouted Dafydd, his pride hurting almost as much as his back.

"He be right. Come one, come all. I be ready for any of you," said Catws, baring her fists.

But no one dared, until, "What of you, Gethin?" she asked, challenging him with her dark eyes.

Gethin didn't much fancy getting flung unceremoniously to the ground, but he didn't want to look scared, either. Especially not in front of Catws. So, to the other boys' astonishment, he stepped forward.

Catws reached for him and grabbed a fistful of his shirt, telling him to hold on to her dress and try to pull or trip her over. But Catws, it turned out, was slippery as an eel. It would've been easier to get a grip on a piece of wet soap. After Gethin had pulled and pushed for a while, in vain, Catws's right leg shot beneath Gethin's left one and the next thing he knew he was on his back on the ground.

"See? You be no better than me!" laughed Dafydd.

Gethin hauled himself to his feet. But instead of going back to the boys, he stepped towards Catws once more.

"Again," he said, determined. And within seconds he was back on his back on the ground. Then it happened again. And again. But instead of giving up, Gethin persisted, despite the fact that his back and legs were bruising black and blue. Because with every defeat, he was learning the technique. And, when he sensed Catws beginning to tire, he felt strength come from somewhere – like it had on Hallowe'en, when he'd escaped from Nathan and Cai – and in a flash he'd caught her leg and thrown her to the ground.

A deadly silence fell. The other boys were staring open-mouthed, unable to believe their eyes. Then Gethin reached out to help Catws up.

"I hope I didn't hurt you," he said to her.

Catws gripped his hand tightly, for a moment too long. But the others didn't notice – they were still in too much shock.

"No. Not in the least," answered Catws, before rubbing her back and smiling shyly up at him.

~

The sheep were ready to shear ten short days after their dip in the river. It had been a warm, mild spring and early summer, very different to the bleak years just gone, when there'd been hardship and famine. The crops were bountiful, farm animals grazed their fill on rich pasture and there'd be plenty of food for everyone come autumn and winter. Guto and the others were sure by now that all this good fortune was because of Gethin's magical presence in the parish. And, although he knew he should tell them the truth, Gethin quietly enjoyed the attention.

Once the shearing was over, everyone gathered at a farm called Daerwynno where they shared a hearty meal of cawl – a kind of lamb stew – and oat-bread. And after they'd eaten their fill, the stories flowed. Gethin's favourite was the tale of Cadwgan Fawr, who rose against the Normans and conquered them at a battle between Creigiau and Pen-tyrch. Cadwgan's weapon of choice was the fwyell, or the battle axe, and so he became Cadwgan y Fwyell. What's more, Cadwgan's spirit still wandered the slopes of Blaenau Morgannwg, ready to wield his deadly weapon again on behalf of his people.

"It be shame that Cadwcan don't a-wield his battle axe against Richard Edwards," put in Guto, and everyone laughed.

Then, to Gethin's embarrassment, they all called on him to recite aloud from Thomas Jones's Almanac – a sort of year book containing news, farming advice and poetry. Guto had been boasting about how Gethin could read, and now everyone was clamouring to hear him. Reluctantly, Gethin stood up and read a few pages aloud. The language was old-fashioned and unfamiliar and he stumbled in a few places, but he got a warm round of applause for his troubles.

"Gethin speaks English, what's more!" said Guto proudly, when he'd finished.

If they'd been surprised to hear Gethin reading the almanac, they were even more astonished to hear him speak the 'iaith fain' or the 'thin language', and everyone insisted that he retell the story of Cadwgan in English to see how much they'd understand. Not much, it turned out, because only one farmer knew more than a handful of English words.

"What be the use of English, howsoever it be?" said one of the farmhands.

"If you were a-wanting to work with the Englishman, Wmffre Mackworth, over Castell-nedd way, you'd have no choice in the matter. It'd be English you'd speak, and there's the end on it," came the answer from the owner of Daerwynno.

"Why would I be a-wanting to slave in the coal workings, picking at a seam deep underground or smelting copper in some infernal manufactory, when the country about us be so beautiful?" replied the farmhand.

The rest of them agreed that only a fool would move so far from his hearth and home, and that there was no future in these dangerous, dirty industries. And they all agreed too that only Welsh would ever be heard across the hills and valleys of Morgannwg, for long centuries to come. Gethin didn't say a word, but he alone knew that it wouldn't really turn out this way. How would the people of Llanwynno feel if they knew?

The moon was high in the sky by the time the night's celebrations wound to an end. Guto wanted to go up Cefn Gwyngul to look for rabbits, but Gethin told him he'd take Catws home first, her house not being far from the farm.

"You be the master," said Guto, smiling.

And with that Gethin realised, without too much surprise, that he was the leader of his gang of friends now.

16

Sometimes, Gethin liked to wander the district on his own. Although he loved the company of Guto and the rest, there was no privacy to be had in the house at Nyth Brân and sometimes he just wanted a bit of peace and quiet.

That's what he was doing today. He'd been walking aimlessly, thinking of this and that, before realising he was heading for Graig Wen Farm, which stood on the edge of the woods of Craig-yr-hesg. This was the wood he'd landed in, some seven months ago. Without really understanding why, he found himself entering the trees.

He hadn't been near the place since Hallowe'en. Forests were still places of mystery and danger that most people avoided, unless they went in to cut or collect wood. They were places where thieves and cutthroats lurked and, despite what the local priest said, spirits and other frightening beings too.

Beings like the tylwyth teg, or boys from the future, smiled Gethin to himself, stepping into the darkness beneath the trees. But his pace soon slowed. It was as quiet as the grave in here, as if everything was whispering – even the trees – and he didn't want to disturb the silence. As he crept deeper into the wood, he noticed the young trees pushing up towards the light, competing for space. Then he stumbled across a rabbit, caught, strangled, in a snare, its wide-open eyes staring straight at him. He knelt to free it before realising that its gaze was blind and it was stone dead. Someone had set the trap very recently, because the furry body was still soft and warm.

Gethin began to feel uneasy, as if someone was watching him – exactly as he'd felt when they'd been hunting the Boncyn Wyla. Deciding he'd better to leave the woods just in case, he realised he had no idea where the forest started or ended. He was lost in the very heart of it. Then he heard a voice, calling him. A booming voice, echoing through the trees:

"Gethin Tan-y-graig!"

Gethin froze. He looked about him. But there was no one to be seen.

"I hear much about you," thundered the voice again.

As Gethin stared in the direction of the sound, a tree shook before him and a tall, upright old man strode into view. He had a long, white beard and wore a green felt hat on his head. But despite his odd appearance, there was something familiar about him.

"Wh-wh-who are you?" asked Gethin, once he'd found his voice.

"Many names have I. But you may call me the Hen Ŵr y Coed – the Old Man of the Woods." The man approached Gethin. "Once, this land was a carpet of trees, until men felled them, for their own ends. See these slopes? They were one, vast forest, until came man, a-cutting and a-burning for the making of charcoal. But I tell you that worse is to come. Much worse. The trees will disappear from the valleys, every last one of them, and the rivers will run black with coal dust."

Gethin knew that this was true. This had happened during the Industrial Revolution. And although things were much better by the twenty-first century, Gethin knew that people still neglected the environment.

"But how do you know?" asked Gethin.

"Listen, Gethin. Listen carefully, and you'll a-hear the leaves a-rustling the truth on the wind. They tell me also that you be not of this world. And that you be in danger. The bells of Gwynno Church will toll before too long. And you shall rest in the churchyard before the year is out . . . if you do not escape."

"What do you mean?" asked Gethin, panicking now. But the Old Man of the Woods had melted into the trees.

Only then did Gethin realise who the strange old man reminded him of: Gransha.

~

The Old Man's words weighed heavy on Gethin for days. One morning, he felt so anxious that he couldn't eat breakfast.

Noticing this, Guto's mam insisted that he stay at home for the day. Gethin didn't care one way or the other – he wasn't in the mood to do much anyway. He offered to sweep the floor for her and she agreed, on the condition that he give it up if he felt at all tired.

The work was repetitive and soothing, so Gethin felt a little better after a while – until Guto's mam began to scream.

"Good heavens above! Out with you!"

Gethin froze in shock. What on earth was wrong?

"Out!" she shouted again, even louder and, without warning, she tore the broom from his hands. For a moment Gethin was afraid she'd hit him with it, before realising that a bird was flapping about above their heads. It was one of the crow family. Not a jackdaw or a carrion crow, but a huge great raven – its long neck feathers and sharp, curved beak terrifying so close up.

Guto's mam was sweeping the air with the broom, trying to hit at the flailing, black bird. At last, with a harsh *cronk*, it flapped through the door and back outside.

"Thank the Lord!" cried Guto's mam in relief, before falling to her knees and making the sign of the cross over and over, whispering what sounded like an ancient prayer.

When she'd recovered, she explained to Gethin that a bird flying into the house brought great misfortune and that was why she'd begged the Virgin Mary and all the saints to save them. To make matters even worse, crows were symbols of death.

"Worse still yet be a white crow," she added. "If ever you see one, run for your life. It be a message from the other world. Indeed, there be no end to the misfortune that this bird will bring."

"Will the prayer work?" asked Gethin nervously, remembering the raven's sharp beak and black, berry-like eyes.

"We shall see, my boy. We shall see." And with that she gathered him to her and hugged him tightly. When at last she let him go, he could see tears sparkling in her eyes.

~

It was the afternoon of the first day of August, and Gethin was feeding the pigs when he heard the church bells chiming, slowly and gravely. He froze. Here were the bells, then, tolling exactly as the Old Man had foretold. When bells tolled like this it was a death knell – meaning that someone in the parish had died. But this was the first time Gethin had heard them in the middle of the afternoon. He saw Guto's father striding towards him.

"Queen Anne – I'll wager," he told Gethin, crossing himself. "We'll hear enough about it before long. Mark my words, Death fears no man – nor woman neither, my boy. Not even when they be of royal blood."

Now Guto's mam had joined them, her rosy cheeks pale as milk. "The raven. She foretold this," she whispered, full of fear, and Guto's father wrapped his arm around her.

"God rest the queen's soul. Will there be riots, or war?" she asked him.

"If there be such things, we be safe here," he replied.

"I should like to go to the church to pray for Queen

Anne's soul and for God's grace upon us all."

Gethin went with her, realising as they started up the slope that this was the first time in ages he'd been on his own with her. Then he saw that she'd started to cry. He put his arm around her to comfort her, as had Guto's father, though Gethin's arm hardly reached her shoulders. She smiled at him through her tears.

"My beautiful boy."

Gethin was glad to be able to comfort her. After all, she was a mam to him by now.

~

That night, Gethin woke in a cold sweat. The bells were ringing the death knell again. Dong. Dong. Dong. But this time, they weren't tolling for the queen – they were tolling for him. Then they stopped. Not a sound, now. Only the whispers of the family, breathing in their sleep. It must have been a dream. In the darkness, he heard the words of the Old Man of the Woods, echoing softly in his ears, warning him that he was in danger.

But, after a week, the world was still turning. There was a new king on the throne and Gethin hadn't fallen sick or had an accident or anything like that. And when he mentioned the Old Man of the Woods's prophecy, his friend Guto laughed.

"Listen you not to one word that comes from that brain-sickly man's mouth. I told you many a time before now, that he be naught but a poor, confused old creature. Tomos Tyddyn Uchaf be his name. Somewhiles ago – long before I was born – a hard winter killed his family and turned the poor dab stark, raving mad."

Raving mad or not, the Old Man had predicted that the church bells would ring the death knell. And what about the raven? A bad omen, or a meaningless incident? But perhaps if Tomos really *was* just a confused old man, the whole thing was a coincidence.

Gethin tried to cling to that hope because he didn't want to escape, even if he knew how. He had a whole family now and a gang of great friends. Despite all the discomforts and the boring, monotonous food – *oh, for a bag of chips!* – he was happy here. Happier than he'd ever been.

17

"Rh-ys! Rh-ys! Rh-ys!" shouted Gethin and his friends, clapping their hands. Catws was with them too, and she was cheering loudest of all. Hearing their support, Rhys, Ifan Blaenhenwysg's older brother, smiled and raised his hand.

At the farmer's sign, Rhys and four other young men set to cutting hay. Amongst them was Ianto, Richard Edwards's servant, his scarred face twisted with determination. This was a competition to see who was the best haymaker – in other words, who could cut the hay the fastest and gather it neatly using only a reaping hook or sickle – a razor sharp, curved blade with a wooden handle.

To the young people, this was one of the high points of the farming year – one of those times, like shearing, when everybody came together to work and then celebrate at the end of the day. Gethin himself had done more than his share of grass cutting over the summer and had been praised for his hard work. The exercise and the outdoor labour were doing him good, he could tell. He'd just celebrated his fourteenth birthday, and he was pretty sure that he was taller than one and a half metres by now, though he had no way of measuring himself. What's more, his body had started to change – he was developing muscles.

The haymaking competition was also a welcome chance for local farmers to bet on the winner, and there was a lot of money riding on this one. Rhys had been in front from the very beginning, by a hair's breadth. Close on his heels was his only serious contender – Ianto. The rumour was that Richard Edwards had been so sure of his man that he'd bet a small fortune on him to win.

Swish. Swish. Swish. The competitors' reaping hooks shone in the sun as they swept through the hay, felling it neatly to one side. It was still touch and go between Rhys and Ianto, but Rhys was still a nose ahead. Then, as the crowd roared their support, the gap between them began to widen slowly.

It was at that point that, without warning, the handle of Rhys's sickle snapped in two and he stopped, abruptly. Everyone fell silent.

What had happened was this. Earlier in the day, unbeknownst to anyone, Richard Edwards had split Rhys's reaping hook to make sure that his favourite, Ianto, would win, allowing him to sweep up all the money. Now, ever the gentleman, Richard Edwards stepped over to offer Rhys another sickle. Thanking him, Rhys set to with even greater determination, and soon the hay was falling again as he swept through the field.

"Rhy-ys! Rhy-ys! Rhy-ys!" shouted Gethin and the others, even louder.

But Richard Edwards had another trick up his sleeve. Although Rhys was giving it his all, the blade on this new reaping hook was so blunt that all he could do was hack at the hay instead of slicing through it neatly. There was no hope now of him beating Ianto and, sure enough, Ianto finished before him to win the contest.

Gethin and his friends couldn't believe what they'd just seen. But Richard Edwards was crowing with delight and Ianto, who was sweating like a pig, sneered over at Rhys's supporters. As Richard Edwards and Ianto congratulated each other, a furious Rhys showed the other farmers the blunt sickle he'd been given by the squire. The farmers were incensed, but there wasn't a lot they could do about it. They had no way of proving that Richard Edwards had played dirty.

"Boo! Cheat! Cur! Scurvy knave!" shouted Gethin and the gang, once they realised what'd happened.

Ianto laughed, showing a row of crooked teeth – as crooked as his spiteful smirk. Ifan was so furious that he ran at Richard Edwards and tried to kick him, but thankfully someone grabbed him and stopped him in time.

"'Twas my brother that won! Not Ianto! My brother!" he yelled.

"Nay, little Ifan. 'Twas Ianto that won," insisted Richard Edwards. "But, if there be any man present who'd fain lose more money in another contest – let him speak now. Come one, come all, I say!" And, with a mocking smile, he pocketed the money.

~

Richard Edwards's arrogant, insulting attitude had enraged everyone. But how on earth could they get their revenge on him? The answer came when Gethin saw Guto sprinting down the lane after a calf that'd escaped one of Nyth Brân's fields. How about Guto challenging Richard Edwards to a cross-country race?

Guto wasn't sure, at first. Could he really beat an adult? But after Gethin promised to teach him tylwyth teg secrets of speed, Guto agreed. These were little white lies, of course – actually, what Gethin planned to do was use the techniques he'd learned from his running magazines.

~

In the courtyard of Plas Coch, Richard Edwards's hunting hounds were barking so loudly he had trouble hearing what Gethin and Guto were saying. Ianto was hovering nearby, and Richard Edwards yelled at him:

"Ianto, man – silence those hounds, if you value your life. Beat them, if needs be – or you'll feel the sting of my own whip."

Glaring suspiciously at the boys, Ianto sloped off to deal with the dogs as Richard Edwards scratched his head, eyeing

Gethin and Guto as he considered their offer.

"Very well. If I lose, you may take my best cow. What manner of thing can you offer me?"

Gethin and Guto looked at each other. They hadn't thought about this. Of course, they couldn't offer anything from their farm without discussing it with Guto's father first.

Richard Edwards laughed. "So," he sneered, "I see how the land lies. Nyth Brân be too poor and lowly a farm to provide a prize worthy of the likes of me. Then will I tell you the prize. If I do win the race, you, Gethin, shall come to Plas Coch and work here as my servant."

"Very well," answered Gethin, without hesitation.

The man stared at him in surprise.

"You be very sure of yourself, my boy."

Gethin didn't say a word. He just smiled and reached out his hand for Richard Edwards to shake. This time, the man said nothing about Gethin behaving like a *gentleman*. Without another word, he stalked back into his grand house and slammed the door. Guto turned to Gethin.

"Know you what you're a-doing?" he asked, nervously.

"Yes," answered Gethin, "I do." Guto had an exceptional talent, a talent that Guto himself hadn't realised yet. No one had. Except for Gethin.

~

Guto collapsed on to the ground in a sweaty heap, his mouth opening and closing like a goldfish that'd jumped out of its bowl. Gethin passed him a bottle of water and Guto gulped thankfully, before bending double and throwing up.

"What . . . be you a-doing to me . . . I be dying . . ." moaned Guto, his face turning a strange shade of purple.

"You'll be fine in a minute. You managed to do ten this time – well done, Guto!" said Gethin, encouragingly.

He'd drawn up a rigorous training programme for Guto, using some of the very latest techniques. One that Guto particularly hated was running as fast as he could up a steep slope, over and over again, with only a short break between each lap. At first, he'd only managed to do it five times. But by now he could do double that. And, though Guto complained, Gethin was sure this exercise would pay back a hundredfold.

"That's enough for today," announced Gethin.

"Thank goodness for that," said Guto, dragging himself to his feet.

"Ready?" asked Gethin.

"A-ready," answered Guto, before yelling: "One. Two. Three!"

Then Guto threw himself down the slope, Gethin hard on his heels. Running down a slope properly – without tripping – was an important part of a runner's skill-set, as well as being a lot more fun than running uphill. But it could be dangerous too. At first, Gethin had been very cautious when he'd raced down slopes after Guto. But by now he'd learned to trust in his body and relax, letting legs carry him, speeding, down the hillside.

"Wheeeee!" shouted Guto.

"Woooow!" yelled Gethin even louder, his legs moving so fast he couldn't even feel them. He felt like he was flying, and a strange sound came to his ears. Was it a sheep, bleating insanely, or a flock of cackling birds? No. It was his own, uncontrollable laughter.

Gethin was still laughing when they reached the river Rhondda, and even Guto had the giggles too by now – until he hit the water. This was how they ended each training session – with Guto standing waist deep in the river to help his muscles recover quickly.

"Good God! The water be glacial today!" cried Guto, his teeth chattering.

"You'll be sleeping on the farmyard heap again tonight. That'll warm your muscles up all right," said Gethin. This was another essential part of the training programme – the combination of the fresh, night air and the heat of the heap restored and built up tired muscles.

"I thank you very much," said Guto sarcastically. Guto still didn't understand why he had to sleep on the heap – a mound of cow-manure and bedding straw – and was terrified the others would find out and make fun of him.

"Don't worry. Your secret's safe with me. Unless, of course, you stink so much that everyone finds out anyway," said Gethin, grinning.

Guto splashed at him, but Gethin was safely on the bank and jumped back out of the way. Guto tried again, this time losing his balance and falling back into the water. But instead of complaining, he gave a shout of joy and started to swim.

"Come on in!" he yelled.

Gethin hesitated. But only for a moment. Tearing off his clothes he threw himself into the river, flipping over to swim on his back. The cold sent a thrill through his blood. He could feel his heart beating strongly and every bit of his body tingled with sensation. *This is how it feels to be completely alive and well*, thought Gethin. It was an incredible feeling.

18

The story of the race had spread like wildfire through the whole parish and far beyond. So the boys weren't surprised to see hundreds of excited people turning up to watch it, especially as it was a beautiful, Michaelmas day. But though the sun shone brightly it wasn't too hot and, as the ground was still dry, conditions were perfect for the race. Despite this, Gethin could tell that Guto was nervous, so he suggested he stretched and warmed up his muscles so he could concentrate better on the task ahead.

Weeks earlier, Guto had finally told his father about the race. And he'd been furious – not just because the boys had organised the whole thing without asking his advice but because he didn't trust Richard Edwards one inch. He warned Guto and Gethin that the squire would be sure to play dirty. But Gethin had such faith in Guto's running ability he was confident they'd be able to cope with any skulduggery Richard Edwards threw their way.

The race was five miles long and the course was defined by a series of posts marked with arrows to show the way, heading down lanes and over fields. It was scheduled to start at five in the afternoon and the farmer from Daerwynno – a rich man, and the only one in the parish, apart from Richard Edwards, to own a pocket watch – was standing at the starting post, ready to give the signal for the race to begin. But though Guto was jumping on the spot like a coiled spring, there was no sign of Richard Edwards – though it was nearly five. Had he got cold feet? The answer came when, at five o'clock on the dot, he trotted up on his horse, Ianto trailing behind him.

"Be you a-ready for the race?" Richard Edwards sneered at Guto.

"Aye – once it pleases you to get down from your horse," he answered.

"Then you'll be a-waiting a long time, my boy – for on the back of this horse I'm a-taking part."

A murmur spread through the crowd, like the buzzing of angry bees.

"Get you down from that horse, this instant," cried Guto's father.

"Spake your son naught of how I was to take part," was Richard Edwards's answer. Behind him, Ianto began to snigger, relishing every moment.

Another wave of angry muttering swept the crowd.

"No problem," said Gethin loudly, surprising everyone.

Ianto stopped sniggering and turned to stare at Gethin. Gethin took no notice. He'd just remembered the story of Guto beating a man on horseback when he was older and he felt sure his talented friend was fast enough to do the same thing at fourteen, too.

"But if Guto wins, you must give us two cows, not one," he added.

"And what will I have if he loses?"

"Me," answered Gethin. "I'll move from Nyth Brân to be a full-time servant to you."

"Nay!" shouted Guto's father.

Richard Edwards ignored his cry. From high up on his horse, he addressed Guto. "Will you accept the challenge?"

It was obvious that Guto didn't know what to say, so Gethin whispered in his ear, "Don't worry. You'll win this race. I'll enchant you with the magic of the tylwyth teg."

Guto had as much faith in Gethin's ability as Gethin had in his. And so he smiled and agreed at once.

Ifan, Siencyn, Dafydd and Catws wished Guto good luck and everyone crossed themselves and said quiet prayers. Then the crowd fell silent as the Daerwynno farmer lifted his handkerchief then dropped it to the ground. The race had begun and Guto shot off like a streak of lightning.

"Not too fast!" Gethin yelled after him. Guto was some hundred meters away already – but Richard Edwards had not moved from the starting line.

"Every success to the boy. I shall catch him in the end, of course," he said, before trotting away, leisurely, on his horse.

There was something in Richard Edwards's sneering arrogance that worried Gethin, and he suspected foul play.

So he headed for the halfway marker, keeping a sharp lookout for any skulduggery. Then he spied Ianto in the distance. Narrowing his eyes, he watched the small man and saw that he was twisting one of the marker poles so that the arrow pointed in a different direction. Then Ianto hid, lurking behind a hedge, until Guto had passed the post and headed off in the wrong direction. After that Ianto sneaked back and turned the post back the right way.

So. Gethin had been right to suspect the worst.

Now he had no choice but to catch Guto and get him back on course. He sprinted hell for leather – faster than he'd ever run before. All the training he'd worked out for Guto had improved his own fitness because in no time he'd cut across three fields – hurdling dykes and hedges as he went – to reach Guto.

"Wait, Guto! Wait!" he shouted, gasping for breath.

Thankfully, Guto heard him and slowed his pace. As swiftly as he could, Gethin explained what he'd seen. Nodding briefly, Guto took off once more – in the right direction this time – and Gethin breathed a huge sigh of relief.

Thanks to his dirty tricks Richard Edwards and his horse were now far ahead, but Gethin decided that two could play at this game. Sprinting ahead to the next marker he twisted it, just as Ianto had, so that the arrow pointed off in a different direction. Then he hid behind a hedge and, as soon as Richard Edwards had passed on horseback, heading way off course, Gethin twisted it back to its original position. A minute or two later, Guto came racing past Gethin, grinning from ear to ear. And by the time Richard Edwards realised what had happened, the race was almost at an end.

A mighty roar rose from the crowd when Guto came into view, bounding down the hill towards the finishing post – and another shout, less enthusiastic, when Richard Edwards came galloping down behind him, mercilessly whipping his horse.

When Guto heard the crowd, he raised his head and lost his balance on the steep slope. Falling, he rolled headlong, before slamming into a stone and coming to a sudden halt. Then he glanced up, dazed. Behind him, Richard Edwards was making ground quickly.

"Get up, Guto Nyth Brân! Remember my promise!" yelled Gethin from the winning post, and with his hand he drew the shape of a circle in the air. Gethin's words and this magical symbol spurred Guto on. Staggering to his feet, he began to run again. But would this last effort be enough to beat Richard Edwards, who was galloping towards him, closing the distance between them with every stride? Now the horse was only metres behind him. And now they were neck and neck as they sprinted for the finishing line. Then, with superhuman effort, Guto hurled himself over the line, seeming to fly through the air as he crossed it, two brief seconds before Richard Edwards.

The crowd went wild, exactly as if Gareth Bale or Aaron Ramsey had scored for Wales. Farmers hefted Guto on to their shoulders and broke into loud song as he bounced above them. But Richard Edwards wasn't watching these celebrations. Instead, he was staring daggers at Gethin. It was obvious he knew what Gethin had done but it was also clear there was no point complaining, because if he did his own scam would come to light.

"I bid you congratulations, Guto," said Richard Edwards,

through gritted teeth. "And your worthy assistant, Gethin Tan-y-graig."

"He be not Gethin Tan-y-graig, mark you," said Guto. "He be Gethin Nyth Brân."

Hearing this, Gethin felt his heart swell with pride. Then Richard Edwards reached down from his horse to offer his hand to Guto and then to Gethin. As he shook hands with Gethin, he leant to whisper in his ear:

"You shall pay dearly for this, sirrah."

No one but Gethin heard these bitter words. But before he could react, the whole crowd was yelling out,

"Long live Gethin Nyth Brân!"

Gethin couldn't enjoy the moment as he should've done, because Richard Edwards's threat was echoing in his head. In the distance, he saw the squire raise his whip then bring it down, hard, on to a cowering Ianto, before lugging him by the ear with one hand and leading the horse with the other in the direction of Plas Coch.

Gethin couldn't even enjoy the sight of Ianto getting his just desserts. Because he knew, all too well, that if Richard Edwards got his way this was just the sort of treatment Gethin himself could expect. Or maybe even worse.

19

The Nyth Brân family were on their way to church again, this time to celebrate the Feast of the parish's patron saint – Gwynno.

Gethin was looking forward to seeing everyone – everyone except Richard Edwards, of course. And Ianto. Catws wouldn't be at the service itself of course, but her parents were letting her join the games afterwards on this special day.

Walking side by side with Guto's mam, Gethin realised that they were about the same height now – he must have grown even taller. And no surprise – by now he'd been living in the past for almost a whole year. Dydd Gŵyl Gwynno was celebrated on the twenty-sixth of October, so there were now only a few days until Hallowe'en.

After the service, the ground in front of the church was packed with people. The piper struck up a tune and many of the youngsters joined in the dance as older people smiled and nodded to the music, remembering the time, long ago, when they themselves had danced with their beloveds.

A wooden ball appeared from somewhere. Guto grabbed it out of the air and threw it at Gethin. As he leapt to catch it, someone snatched the ball from his hands. Richard Edwards.

"The game be up for you, sirrah," he sneered. But Guto's father had been watching, and strode straight over.

"Happy St Gwynno's Day to you," Richard Edwards greeted him, smirking. "But I fear this be not a happy day for the boy." He pointed at Gethin.

"No, indeed," he went on. "For, being as I am a gentleman of means, I have truck with many merchants, far and wide across the land. Even, mark you, as far as Aberhonddu. And thus I can tell you, Father Nyth Brân, on good authority, that there be no such farm of the name Tan-y-graig near Llanfrynach, nor anywhere within that parish. So from whither came this boy, in truth? And how, indeed, can such a poor, lowly creature converse so well in English? Truly, I hear tell he speaks a word or two even of the French tongue! Perchance he is a spy, come to sow seeds of dissent amongst us?"

Attracted by his loud voice, others were gathering to listen. Gethin felt as if the world was closing in on him. He saw Guto's father staring at him in disbelief and his stomach sank to his knees . . . but there was worse to come.

"But, and this be of far greater importance, Ianto saw him a-stealing a ram."

"Gethin would never do such a thing," said Guto's father, placing his arm around Gethin protectively.

"So you say. There be but one way to settle this. Go we to your fields, and we shall see what we shall see."

Reluctantly, Guto's father agreed, leading Gethin through the crowd. As Gethin left the church's grounds, his legs shaking in fear, the last person he saw was Catws, who'd just arrived. As long as he lived, he'd never forget the way her smile froze when she realised that something was terribly wrong.

By the time they reached Nyth Brân Guto had joined them, having run the whole way home to support his friend –

despite the fact that his father had warned him to stay at the church.

"Were he a son of mine, he'd know to mark my words," said Richard Edwards scornfully.

"He be not your son, and I thank God for that," Guto's father retorted.

Then began the search for the ram. By now, Gethin was trembling from his head to his toes. Although he hadn't stolen the animal, he was terrified that Richard Edwards would somehow get the better of him. They went from one field to the next, fields that Gethin knew like the palm of his hand by now. Fields with names like Dan y Ffynnon – Beneath the Spring; Waun Dan Sgubor – the Heath Below the Barn; Hendra – Old Place and Cae Isha Erfin – Lower Turnip Field. There was no sign of the ram anywhere. Gethin noticed Richard Edwards's eyes shifting, uneasily. Then he saw Ianto walking towards them, smirking.

"Master! I have seen the ram! Down by the river there!"

They all rushed down the slope to the river Rhondda. And there, on the wooded edge of Waun Glandŵr, was Richard Edwards's ram, grazing contentedly.

"Upon my word," said Guto's father, in surprise.

"Stole not Gethin the ram!" Guto protested.

"There be the proof," said Richard Edwards, indicating the ram. "And there the witness." He pointed at Ianto.

"Truly, Master. Saw I everything," said Ianto, throwing a victorious smile in Gethin's direction. It was obvious to everyone that he was lying. But how could they prove otherwise?

"Know you that the punishment for such a crime is to hang by the neck?" Richard Edwards asked Gethin, as nonchalantly as if he was chatting about the weather.

"Hang?" whispered Gethin.

"Nay, Gethin, lad. We'll not see you hang," said Guto's dad, putting a comforting hand on his shoulder. Turning to Edwards he said, "Surely there be some way we may reach accord in this matter?"

Richard Edwards looked at Gethin for a moment or two before answering.

"Despite what some might say of me, I be not an unreasonable man. Seeing that Gethin already offered his service to me, at the time of the race . . ."

There was no need for him to finish the sentence. Gethin knew his fate by now, and the horror of it was almost too terrible to bear. With a heavy heart, Guto's father agreed to free Gethin from his duties at Nyth Brân after Hallowe'en. Richard Edwards left Nyth Brân in satisfaction with Ianto turning to tag behind him – after glaring spitefully at Gethin.

Gethin felt like throwing up. He was to be servant to the most hateful person in the whole parish – perhaps in the whole of Morgannwg. But however disheartened Gethin was, he also knew he'd had a lucky escape. If Richard Edwards had insisted, Gethin could have faced something far worse.

~

Gethin spent that afternoon wandering Nyth Brân's fields on his own. He didn't want company. In his hand he held the smooth stone Guto had given him almost a year ago, with the map of the parish scratched on its surface. As he fingered it, he thought about his options. His first reaction had been to try to escape from Richard Edwards. But to where? Then he'd done his best to convince himself that things wouldn't be as bad as they seemed. After a year or two, perhaps there'd be some way to come back to Nyth Brân – *If you live, that is,* whispered a voice in his ear. The voice of the Hen Ŵr y Coed – the Old Man of the Woods. Gethin looked about him, but there was no one to be seen. What if the Old Man was right, and he'd be lying, dead, in the church cemetery before a year was out?

Trying to put these thoughts from his head, he studied the map on the stone. He frowned. There was something odd about it. What was it? Then he realised. There was not one but two faces on it. The first, the one that Guto had carved, looked towards the east. But there was another face there too – staring westwards. A terrifying face. The face of the devil.

A shiver ran through him. He had to escape, or he'd die. And the only person who could help him was the person who'd warned him of his fate, long weeks ago.

~

The sky was blue-black and the wind whined sharply as Gethin reached the edge of Craig-yr-hesg wood. He paused before venturing into the trees and heading for the depths of the forest.

"Hello-o!" he called, over and over, using his hands as a loudspeaker. His voice echoed through the forest, the sound bouncing back at him across the rocks. Then, at long last, Gethin heard a familiar voice from behind him.

"Came you at last. I have been expecting you."

The Old Man walked towards him. For someone so ancient, he moved surprisingly fast. Gethin had never felt so glad to see him.

"I need your help," he blurted. But before he could say any more, the Old Man raised a hand to silence him.

"I know everything. If you had but listened to me, you could have escaped back to the present during the summer, on the night before Gŵyl Ifan, the Feast of Saint John's Eve, when time's door be ajar. There be but one more chance for you yet – if you be brave enough to take it."

"When?" asked Gethin, desperately.

"Noswyl Calan Gaeaf, of course," came the answer.

Hallowe'en.

"But that's tomorrow night!" cried Gethin.

"Exactly so. Go you directly to the place you arrived at. I will show it to you."

The Old Man began to walk away but Gethin remained frozen on the spot. He was still in shock.

"Make haste! There be no time to lose," said the Hen Ŵr y Coed.

Somehow, Gethin managed to put one foot before the other to follow him into the very heart of the wood.

20

"How shall I fare without you?" cried Guto, his eyes filled with pain, when Gethin told him about the plan to escape from this world. "I don't understand. Why can you not cast a spell upon Richard Edwards?"

Gethin paused before answering. Then he made up his mind. He couldn't live with the lie any longer – the time had come for him to tell Guto the truth.

"Because . . . I'm not one of the tylwyth teg," said Gethin.

Guto stared at him in astonishment.

"Then what be you?" he whispered.

"A person. Just like you. But . . ." Gethin hesitated.

"But what?"

"But . . . I come from the future. Three hundred years in the future, to be exact."

Guto began to laugh. He'd been happy to believe Gethin was one of the tylwyth teg, but the idea that someone could appear from the future was completely beyond him.

"Came you on the night of Calan Gaeaf! Of course you be of the tylwyth teg," he insisted.

"But there are other times of the year when spirits wander at night, aren't there?" asked Gethin.

"Yes, of course. As know you well yourself. The nights of Calan Mai – Midsummer – and Gŵyl Ifan – the Feast of Saint John," replied Guto.

Then Gethin told him that the Old Man of the Woods wasn't crazy after all, but a wise man, a seer – someone who understood the natural world and all its secrets. Someone who'd explained to him that the boundaries between the past, present and future were as thin as eggshells on these special nights. And that's how he'd been able to cross time's boundary when he'd arrived here, a year ago tomorrow.

"He told me I have to escape this Hallowe'en, or I'll be in terrible danger," he added.

But Guto still wouldn't believe him.

"Right," said Gethin. "Then I'll have to prove it to you. Are the clothes I was wearing when I arrived still here somewhere?"

"They are. I hid them, in the cowshed," answered Guto.

They hurried to the cowshed, where Guto found the sack and handed it to Gethin. Gethin delved inside and pulled out the wig with the big ears and the furry slippers. Guto reached out to touch them, fingering them in astonishment. He'd never seen anything plastic before, but at least he could tell that they weren't real flesh.

"See?" said Gethin. "They were fancy dress. Something people wear for fun, in the future. I was at a fancy-dress party before I disappeared on Hallowe'en."

"A party?" asked Guto, not understanding.

"A celebration. A Hallowe'en celebration. Up on Graig Wen."

"Graig Wen Farm?" asked Guto in surprise.

"Not exactly. A part of Pontypridd that's named after the farm."

"Pont y tŷ pridd? On the banks of the Taf? But . . . there be but one or two cottages there, that be all."

"A town will grow there, you'll see."

"A big one?"

"That depends what you mean by big. About thirty thousand people."

"Ten and twenty thousand!" exclaimed Guto.

"That's nothing. Caerdydd is ten times bigger than that."

"Caerdydd?"

"Yeah. The capital of Cymru."

"Cymru has a *capital*?" asked Guto, more incredulous than ever. Now there was no stopping him – he bubbled over with a million and one questions about the future but, though he begged Gethin to answer them, the Old Man of the Woods had warned Gethin not to say anything, in case he upset the balance of his own time.

"Sorry. I can't tell you any more."

"Tell me but one little thing . . ." begged Guto.

Gethin gave in. "OK. You'll be famous throughout Cymru as the fastest runner that's ever been, and you'll win many races – in fact, you'll win every race you run in."

"Me? A famous runner?" gasped Guto. "Do you speak the truth?"

"I do."

"Upon your life?"

"Upon my life."

A smile spread across Guto's face then he began to jump up and down in excitement, clapping his hands. Gethin did his very best to look happy for him, but his heart was bleeding because he also knew that one day Guto would collapse after a race and die, a young man. Even if he'd been allowed to tell him the whole truth, Gethin would never have done so.

When Guto had calmed down, he turned to his friend. "But . . . are you not happy here?"

"Yes. Course I am."

"Why do you want to escape, then?"

"No 'want to' about it. *Got to* escape."

"But why?"

"Because if I don't, I won't be here this time next year. The Old Man of the Woods told me if you stay longer than one year in another time dimension you can never get back."

"Whither will you be then?"

"Resting in the cemetery, up at the church. That's where. So, will you help me work out what to tell everyone?"

With a heavy heart, Guto agreed. Gethin heaved a sigh of relief. This was hard enough as it was. Leaving on bad terms with Guto would've been unbearable.

21

Gethin had a lump in his throat as he said goodbye to Ifan, Dafydd and Siencyn, telling them he was fleeing to the safety of relatives in America, far from the clutches of Richard Edwards. He wasn't looking forward to saying farewell to the Nyth Brân family either, but first of all there was someone else he had to face: Catws.

He found her scrubbing clothes in a stream near her home. When she looked up and saw him coming towards her, she dropped the clothes in the water and ran to him.

"I have been so worried about you! Be it true that you are to become servant to that terrible man?"

Gethin had planned to tell her the truth about everything, but when he saw her anxious face, he couldn't say a word. This made Catws worry even more.

"Say you something!"

"I'm leaving, Catws. To go to relatives, who live far away," he said, repeating the lie he'd told the rest of the gang.

"But will you return?" asked Catws, quietly.

"Of course," answered Gethin. He couldn't tell her the truth. It was too painful, for he knew he'd never see her again. Not in this world, anyway.

"At least Guto will remind me of you while you be away," said Catws. Then she laughed to see the confusion on Gethin's face.

"You two are like to peas in a pod. Every day you grow more alike. Know you not?"

Gethin hadn't noticed how similar he was to Guto. And no wonder, without a mirror.

He stayed for a bit then, to help Catws wring out the wet clothes. The sopping material was freezing cold and Catws's hands were red. Suddenly Gethin saw tears tumble down her cheek.

"It be that old wind, a-making them water," said Catws, drying her eyes. But they both knew that that was a lie. As they said farewell, neither one could look the other in the eye.

~

On the way back to Nyth Brân, Gethin walked past Gwynno Church and looked up towards the slopes of Cefn Gwyngul. In the weak, late-afternoon light, the bracken on the slope glowed rusty red.

He decided to pay one last visit to the church's cemetery, and saw for the first time how many children were buried here – some no more than babies a few months old. Stopping before the grave of a fourteen-year-old boy, he wondered just how he'd died. Had it been an illness? If it was, he thought, there'd probably be a cure for it in three hundred years' time. He put out his hand to touch the grave stone. It felt icy cold, as cold as the water in the stream. If he hadn't decided to escape back to the present, perhaps soon he would also rest in this cemetery and his friends would come to visit his grave. If the Old Man of the Woods was to be believed, that is.

Trying to distract himself, he thought about the farewell feast that awaited him at Nyth Brân. It wouldn't be 'spoon food' for supper tonight – not the usual porridge or gruel – but proper, tasty food. Guto's mam had promised to prepare 'pastai neithior' – delicious pasties made for special occasions from mutton, onions and mixed herbs. She'd also said she'd make Gethin's favourite dessert – posset, a pudding of hot milk and beaten egg yolks with plenty of sugar on top. Usually, she only made posset when one of the family was ill.

Gethin could taste the posset already and he imagined taking a big spoonful of it and savouring the sweet pudding in his mouth before swallowing it slowly. The feeling was so real that he didn't notice the two figures rushing towards him – until it was too late.

"Gethin Nyth Brân! Or, should I say 'Gethin, Servant of Richard' . . ."

The posset flew from Gethin's mind.

"Ifan Blaenhenwysg was never a one to hold his tongue. I know all about your plan to break your vow and flee to America. Let me tell you this, sirrah. There be no escaping me."

Before Gethin could react, Ianto threw a sack over his head, tying it with rope and dragging him on to the back of Richard Edwards's horse. But not before throwing in a few sly kicks and punches as he did so. Everything happened so fast and Ianto was so very strong that Gethin had no chance to defend himself. Richard Edwards was right. There was no escaping him.

~

Gethin wasn't sure exactly how long he'd been kept prisoner in the stone pigsty at Plas Coch, but it had been dark outside for quite a while now. He had, perhaps, four or five hours left till midnight, and then it would be too late: the door of time would slam shut – for ever.

Gethin shivered with fear as the sudden barking of Richard Edwards's dogs broke the deadly silence. Then he heard a scratching on the hut's door. As he pressed himself, fearfully, into the far corner, he heard the door creak slowly open. And through the dim light he saw, not an enemy, but his best friend.

"Quick! Take you off your clothing!" hissed Guto, slipping off his own shirt. "Put mine on. In the darkness, Richard Edwards will think you be me. Then I will lead him a merry dance and lose him in the marshland beyond the church."

Gethin was speechless with gratitude. He knew that Guto was afraid to venture out on Hallowe'en, yet he'd been brave enough to leave Nyth Brân and run through the darkness to Plas Coch to save his friend. As they exchanged clothes, Guto explained that Catws had followed Gethin after they'd met at the stream because she'd wanted to say goodbye properly, and she'd seen everything. After that she'd run the whole way to Nyth Brân and told Guto what had happened. While Guto's father had taken her home – for it wasn't safe for a girl to be out on her own tonight, of all nights – Guto had sneaked out and made the perilous journey to Plas Coch.

Before he said farewell, Guto handed Gethin a bundle – his Hobbit costume.

"Perchance you'll need this too," said Guto. Though it was dark, Guto's wide smile shone out.

"Thank you," said Gethin, "for saving me."

"There be no need for thanks. You be a brother to me, Gethin Nyth Brân – now and for always. I will never forget you," said Guto. Then he disappeared into the darkness.

The sound of barking exploded through the blackness of the night once more. It was time to go. Gethin crept out of the hut and ran, hell for leather, down the path to the gate, before turning right down the lane in the direction of Llantrisant.

Before long the moon peeped from behind the clouds to

light his path and prevent him from tripping up on the stony track. He tried to concentrate on his breathing and to take light, regular strides, instead of sprinting wildly and tiring quickly. The wind got up, pushing him backwards, but he battled onwards against it.

Over the cry of the wind Gethin heard horses, many of them, galloping in the distance. Soon he realised, with fear, that the sound was closing in on him. Hurling himself over a hedge, he crouched behind a large stone and tugged off his clothes, though the cold wind froze his bare skin. Then he pulled on his Hobbit costume. And waited.

When Richard Edwards and his men came galloping round the corner, Gethin mounted the stone and roared as loudly as his lungs could manage. The horses reared and screamed in fear. But, for the men, what stood before them was not a teenager in fancy dress but some hideous phantom, unleashed from the underworld on Hallowe'en. They fell into as much panic as the horses and Richard Edwards was thrown from his saddle. By the light of the moon, Gethin saw that Ianto's sour, scarred face was paralysed by terror. This was Gethin's only chance and he seized it, feverishly sprinting away.

In no time he'd left the main road and was racing down a path towards Graig Wen Farm. In front of him, he could see the outlines of trees and rocks in the moonlight – the woods of Craig-yr-hesg. He was almost there. Almost safe. Soon he'd left the path to cross the fields in the direction of the wood.

But when he reached the edge of the trees the sound of a firing gun exploded, echoing across the rocks and freezing him on the spot. Then the hate-filled voice of Richard Edwards came to his ears, carried by the wind.

"You cannot make a fool out of me, Gethin! Neither can you escape me, you hear?"

Next came Ianto's vicious sneer, promising that if Richard Edwards didn't shoot him first, Ianto would throw a rope round Gethin's neck and hang him then and there. Gethin's legs felt like jelly. He realised that one of his Hobbit's ears had fallen off – they must have found the fake ear and guessed the rest. He felt tears welling, then he gave himself a stern talking-to. This wasn't the time to despair.

So he turned and ran, ducking through the trees, in the direction of the magical glade. He could hear the shouts and hooves closing in on him from behind. Any moment now, they'd be upon him. Then, without warning, a thick mist fell. Now Gethin had no idea where he was going – until he felt a strong hand grip his arm and, before he could scream, another across his mouth.

"Follow me," whispered the Hen Ŵr y Coed – the Old Man of the Woods.

Gethin ran in step behind the Old Man, who moved like someone quarter his age. The mist was beginning to clear – enough for him to realise he was standing in the middle of a perfect circle of oak trees. He'd made it. He turned to thank the Old Man, but there was no one there. The Hen Ŵr y Coed had melted into the mist.

Then Gethin heard branches snapping. Through the last wisps of the mist he saw Richard Edwards striding towards him, a malicious grin on his face and a gun in his hand – its muzzle pointing directly at him. Instinctively, Gethin hurled himself to the ground a second before the flash of the gun caught him, the shot deafening him. He felt a hard blow to his side and the most terrible burning. The bullet had hit him.

Then the mist cleared. He saw the stars, lined up in a perfect row. And then everything went dark.

PART 3

22

Gethin opened his eyes. Darkness. Still. He tried to move his arm, his hand, his fingers. But for some reason his body wasn't listening to him. *Maybe I've died*, he thought.

Then he heard a sound in the distance. *I must be alive after all, or my ears wouldn't be working.* Concentrating on the sound he realised it was dogs, barking – approaching at speed. It had to be Richard Edwards's hunting hounds. Soon they'd leap on him and tear him to pieces like a helpless hare.

Now he was shaking from head to toe and his teeth were chattering uncontrollably. Desperately, he tried to control his body and lie still, praying the dogs wouldn't find him. But above the sound of his clattering teeth he could hear the barking growing ever closer.

Through the darkness he saw the form of some huge, fur-covered beast, leaping at him. He felt its sour breath, hot on his cheek. He tried to wrench his head away, but there was no escape. The monster opened wide its maw, revealing pin sharp teeth . . . before putting out a great pink tongue and licking Gethin's face. After a moment or two, Gethin realised that it wasn't trying to tear him apart. It was trying to be friendly.

~

Butty Bach was the dog's name, and Mr Roberts of Trealaw was his owner. Helen, Gethin's mam, told him this after he'd come round in hospital, two days earlier. By the time Butty Bach and Mr Roberts found him, Gethin had been out all through the night and was frozen to the bone.

"No wonder you got hypothermia," said his mam, who'd been sitting at his bedside the whole time, waiting for him to wake up. Unlike Guto's parents, she didn't believe a word of the Bible, but she'd prayed fervently for Gethin to recover just the same.

"A firework must've hit you, because there are burn marks and a big bruise on your right side," she added, before telling Gethin that he'd spent his first day in hospital slipping in and out of consciousness. He'd been jabbering in some sort of garbled Welsh – because of his high temperature, surely. But she'd understood enough to recognise the name 'Guto' – and she hadn't remembered Gethin mentioning him before.

"Was this Guto with you when you got lost?" she asked.

A little voice in his head told Gethin not to tell his mam the truth.

"No, I don't think so. I don't remember," he whispered.

"You must remember something," she said, in the all-too-familiar forceful voice.

She hasn't softened at all, thought Gethin. *Why can't she be more like Elen, Guto's mam?* But, without realising it, he'd got her wrong. He hadn't seen her tears, or heard her begging him to wake up, or whispering to him that she loved him more than anything in the whole, wide word – because he'd been unconscious.

"Nothing at all?" she asked again.

"No, really – I don't . . ." repeated Gethin, then he began to cough. His throat was so sore he could hardly speak.

His mam handed him a glass of water and helped him swallow a mouthful. "Well?" she persisted.

"I'm tired," answered Gethin. And he meant it.

"Try and get a bit of sleep. Will you be all right if I go and grab a coffee and something to eat? I haven't had anything for hours," said his mam.

"OK," whispered Gethin. That was all he could manage to say.

"You've had a shock, that's all. Everything will be fine, you'll see," she went on. There was an unfamiliar tenderness in her voice. Gethin tried to smile, to look as if he was agreeing with her. He knew it was too soon to know if everything would be 'fine'. Too soon by far. His mam hesitated for a moment, as if she was afraid to leave him, before turning and walking out of the room.

It felt strange to be lying in a real bed. The sheets were so white and the pillow so soft and comfortable. Gethin felt himself sinking lower and lower into the depths of the bed but, though his body felt wiped out, his mind wasn't ready to sleep yet.

If he'd spent a year with Guto, how come he'd been lost for just one night? Had he imagined the whole thing? But Guto was so alive in his memory. And so was Catws. And the others.

And while it was a huge relief to be safe from the clutches of Richard Edwards, he felt so very sad too. Sad that he'd never see Guto again.

But whatever happened, there was a tiny grain of comfort: he knew he'd see Catws once more. And Ifan, Dafydd and Siencyn – or their modern versions, at least.

Then he remembered Ianto. And Nathaniel. And his heart sank at the thought that he'd have to see them again too: as Nathan and Cai.

He sighed, closed his eyes and tried to will himself to sleep.

~

Compared to Nyth Brân, the house seemed so very big, tidy and clean, and the outside world so very noisy and threatening – so much so that Gethin was glad to spend most of his time in his room.

The food was strange as well: too heavy, and too salty or sweet. Gethin had often dreamed of eating chips when he was in Llanwynno. But when he'd done so at last, he'd been unable to eat more than a handful. They were so greasy they turned his stomach.

And though he tried his hardest, even his gecko, Emil, didn't interest him much any more. All he could think about was Guto. And Catws. And his other friends from Llanwynno.

After a week of staying at home to look after him, his mam had to go back to work. Secretly, Gethin had enjoyed having her fussing over him from dawn to dusk. During that time she'd asked him many times who'd attacked him, but Gethin still insisted he had no idea.

As his mam was about to leave the house, the landline rang and she picked it up. It was Caitlin, asking for Gethin. She'd already sent him lots of texts, but he hadn't answered. He had no idea what to say.

When Helen brought the phone up to his room, Gethin shook his head frantically at her. He still didn't want to speak to Caitlin, not after causing so much stress for everyone. So Gethin's mam told her Gethin was still asleep. After she'd hung up, his mam asked him if he'd like to invite Caitlin round over the weekend, before going back to school. Gethin was tempted to say yes, but he didn't feel confident enough to see Caitlin on her own so he refused. And, for once, his mam didn't push it.

When she'd left, Gethin decided to clean Emil's tank. He had to do *something*, or he'd go off his head. As he carefully lifted the gecko from the tank, he heard the front door bell and froze. It had to be Caitlin. His grandfather never usually bothered to answer the door and Gethin prayed he wouldn't this time, either. But before long he heard voices and then Gransha shouting:

"Geth! Your friend's 'ere."

Silence. Then the sound of Caitlin, climbing the stairs. As the door opened, Gethin put Emil back in his tank and tried to look as casual as possible. But his jaw fell when he saw who it was. It wasn't Caitlin after all – but Nathan. Nathan, standing there, smirking at him. He was as big and as menacing as ever. So different to frail, sickly Nathaniel.

Gethin stared at him, open-mouthed.

"You look like you've seen a ghost," said Nathan, before

stepping into the room and closing the door behind him.

Without thinking, Gethin took a step back.

"What's his name, then?" asked Nathan, pointing at the gecko.

"Emil," answered Gethin.

Nathan stepped towards the tank.

"Can I hold him?"

Without waiting for an answer, Nathan stuck his paw-like hand into the tank, swiftly snatching up the little creature.

"He's a cute little thing. Wouldn't want anything to happen to him."

"Like what?" stammered Gethin.

"Like an accident . . . if anyone ever finds out what happened on Hallowe'en."

Suddenly, Gethin's mouth felt as dry as Emil's cage.

"You kept your mouth shut?" asked Nathan.

"Yes."

"And you won't tell no one?"

"No."

Nathan stared at Gethin, and his eyes seemed to pierce right through him. Then, after what seemed an age, still watching Gethin, he slowly placed Emil back in his tank.

"Knew I could depend on you," he said, walking to the door. As he opened it, he turned once more.

"By the way, Caitlin loved the present. Good job."

With that, Nathan disappeared through the door. Gethin stood, stock still, as if his feet were nailed to the floor.

23

Gethin peered through the taxi window. So many people. So many houses. So many cars. And everything moving so quickly. It was making him feel faint. He closed his eyes and imagined seeing Caitlin again. And everyone else. Then he began to feel sick to his stomach. He really wasn't sure if he was ready for this.

Gransha had offered to pay for the taxi as a treat on his first day back at school, and Gethin had been pleased to take him up on it. At least he'd chosen a good day, he thought, because today was the trip to St Fagan's, the National Museum of History. He'd been there once before, years ago when they'd visited Gransha before he'd had trouble walking, and Gethin had loved the place.

He decided to ask the taxi driver to drop him off before they arrived at school. By now Gethin could hear the loud shouts and laughter of schoolkids, just like when he'd gone to the fair at Ynys-y-bŵl. That time, the sound of the fair had reminded him of the school yard.

Someone barged into his back, shoving at his bag.

"Did Mami make you sandwiches for the trip?" asked a mocking voice.

Cai. Gethin couldn't believe his bad luck. Off all the people in the school, why did he have to bump into him first? He turned to face him and watched as Cai's features melted away, turning into Ianto's scarred face. Gethin couldn't help staring, and Cai shifted uneasily.

"What's the matter with you, weirdo?" he sneered, striding past Gethin and barging him aside.

Gethin retreated to the far corner of the yard. All the shouting and leg-pulling and pushing and running was making his head spin. He'd never felt so awkward. He was dying to get back to the peace and quiet of his bedroom, but at the same time he was furious with himself for being so pathetic. *What happened to the confident young man who did so well in Llanwynno?* he wondered. Then he answered himself: *He's far away in the past, that's what. He was another person, in another world.*

Then he saw the Tri Trist standing on the other side of the yard. Like him, they were hoping no one would notice them before the bell went. He decided to head over to them. Anything was better than standing here like a lemon, on his own.

"Hello," said Gethin. He couldn't think of anything else to say. The Tri Trist glanced at him in surprise – they weren't used to anyone speaking to them. Gethin stared back, so amazed at how similar they were to Ifan Blaenhenwysg, Dafydd Penrhiwgwynt and Siencyn Hafod Ucha that he started to laugh. But the boys thought he was making fun of them, and their eyes dimmed as they cowered back into their shells, like soft-bodied crabs escaping a predatory fish. Before Gethin could apologise and give some sort of explanation – he couldn't tell the truth or they'd think he'd gone completely nuts – he saw Caitlin striding past and hurried to catch up with her.

"Caitlin!" he called, out of breath.

Caitlin turned and smiled at him – with Catws's perfect teeth. But everything else about her was so very different from Catws, like a mirror that showed the complete opposite.

"How are you?" she asked.

"Better," replied Gethin.

"You never answered my phone calls," she said, frowning a little.

Gethin blushed, and the words withered in his mouth.

"I was really worried about you, you know," she went on.

"Sorry," said Gethin feebly, looking at his feet.

Then, "See you," she blurted suddenly, hurrying away.

Gethin could've kicked himself. He'd looked forward to seeing Catws so much . . . then he realised that that was the problem. She wasn't Catws – but Caitlin.

Lifting his head, he saw Caitlin and Nathan heading into the school building, their heads so close they were almost touching, laughing together, obviously delighted to be in each other's company. Gethin felt as if someone had thrown a bucket of cold water over him.

"Welcome back to the present," he muttered to himself, with a bitter little sigh.

~

The schoolkids crowded around the Penparcau tollgate in St Fagan's, though some had slunk round the corner to the bakery to buy cheese rolls. It was obvious that Miss Jenkins Hanes – the History teacher – was hungry too, because she said hardly anything about the Rebecca Riots before announcing it was lunchtime.

While most of them flocked back to the canteen in the main building, Gethin headed straight to the straw-thatched house down the lane on the left and walked inside. The room was dark, smoky and comfortless, but Gethin had never felt so at home. He breathed deeply, enjoying the sour smell of smoke mixed with the scents of leather and wood. In his mind's eye he saw Guto's mam by the fireplace, preparing food. Then he stared up towards the croglofft, where the twins had giggled and waved at him. He could hear voices outside. It had to be Guto, with the gang, calling for him to come and hunt rabbits on the slopes of Cefn Gwyngul, or to catch trout with them in the river Rhondda.

Without a second's hesitation he stepped out of the house and into sunlight, to join Guto and the boys. But all he found was Cai, torturing the Tri Trist.

"Do you that once more, you bwbach, and you'll be a-getting a clattering and a half from me!" thundered a strong, commanding voice.

Cai froze. So did the Tri Trist. Gethin looked about to see who'd shouted, before realising that it had been him. He'd used the old dialect of Blaenau Morgannwg. And Cai was staring at him in total disbelief.

"You *what*?" said Cai, striding towards him with narrowed eyes. "You off your head or what?"

Then Cai reached out and grabbed Gethin around the neck. Without thinking, Gethin ducked and swivelled in one smooth movement, throwing Cai to the ground.

Cai lay there, stunned, gaping at Gethin before getting unsteadily to his feet. Gethin stepped towards him, ready to throw him again if he had to. But Cai was already taking a step backwards.

"You really *are* off your head!" he managed, and his voice, for once, shook.

The Tri Trist were still staring at Gethin, open-mouthed, as Cai slunk past them with his head down. Then Cai saw Nathan standing by the gate with Caitlin, and he began to swagger again, obviously expecting a word or two of support from his friend.

But Nathan ignored him completely, turning to Gethin instead. "Not bad. Not bad at all," he told him, with a hint of admiration.

"Whatever," spat back Gethin. "I don't care what you think." He was fired up now, as the spirit of brave, daring, eighteenth-century Gethin exploded through his veins.

"Hope you liked the present – the one you got from Nathan," he shouted at Caitlin.

"How did you know about the present?" she asked.

"Because it was mine. I made it for you."

Caitlin spun to look at Nathan. "Is this true?" she asked.

Nathan didn't say a word. But the disappointment was obvious on Caitlin's face as she turned on her heel and walked away.

"Caitlin, wait!" called Nathan, rushing after her – but not before throwing a Gethin a nasty look.

Bit by bit, the adrenaline was ebbing away. And only then did Gethin realise exactly what he'd done.

~

On the coach back to school, Gethin made sure he sat at the front, close to the teacher, just in case. When Nathan got on the coach, Gethin looked down. He didn't want to provoke him, but he needn't have worried – not yet, at least – because Nathan headed straight to Caitlin, gesturing for the boy in the seat next to her to get lost. The boy shot up at once and Nathan sat down next to Caitlin, who made a point of looking out of the window and ignoring him.

Gethin gave up trying to spy between the seats to see what was going on between them and turned to face the front. He saw the Tri Trist stepping up on to the coach then 'Ifan Blaenhenwysg' sat down next to him, with the other two behind.

"Thanks for rescuing us," said the boy, holding out his hand.

"Bit of a *gentleman*, I see," said Gethin, remembering Richard Edwards's words. The boy smiled nervously, not sure how to answer.

"What's your name?" asked Gethin, shaking his hand.

"Evan," he answered.

"And yours?" Gethin asked the other two.

"Dawid," said the first. "My mam's from Poland," he explained.

Then "Jordan," answered 'Siencyn'.

Before long the boys were eagerly asking Gethin all about himself. Obviously his 'accident' on Hallowe'en and his stay in hospital had been hot gossip in school. And to think Gethin had thought no one ever noticed him!

He soon found himself telling Evan, Dawid and Jordan about his interest in running.

Evan's eyes lit up. "Hey!" he said. "You should take part in the big New Year's Eve race!"

"What race?" asked Gethin.

"Ras Guto Nyth Brân," he answered.

Gethin almost fell out of his seat. This was a sign, if ever there was one! He remembered the thrill of running with Guto. If he'd run as fast as that then, why not do it again, in the present? Then he remembered that he'd beaten Nathan too, when he'd escaped from him on Hallowe'en.

"Great idea!" said Gethin, standing up. The coach had begun its journey back by now and he strode as steadily as he could down the aisle, heading straight for Nathan, who was talking earnestly to Caitlin. The two of them looked up, surprised.

"Ras Guto Nyth Brân. New Year's Eve. You and me," Gethin told him.

"You what?" asked Nathan, frowning in confusion.

"If I win, you leave me alone. For good."

"And if you don't?" asked Nathan, smirking exactly like Richard Edwards.

"Then I'll do anything you ask me to," answered Gethin.

Nathan laughed. It was obvious he thought Gethin didn't have a hope in hell of beating him. And from the astonished look on Caitlin's face, neither did she.

24

Gethin didn't get much sleep that night, with the enormity of the challenge he'd set Nathan lying heavy on his mind. When he dragged himself down to the kitchen for breakfast, his mam had already left to go shopping. But he didn't get much peace, because in no time Gransha came in to make himself a cuppa. As ever, he had something sarky to say:

"*Still live 'ere then, do you?*"

"Looks like it," answered Gethin.

He'd never dare talk like this to his mam, but his tad-cu just laughed, showing the gap between his teeth. Gransha Grange was very different to Gethin. He wasn't afraid of anything, not even death. Robert David Tanner was his full name, but everyone called him Bobby Grange because he'd been a die-hard Cardiff City supporter, standing behind the goal in the stand people called 'The Grange End' until being on his feet for a whole game became too painful for him. He'd been too proud to go to a stand where he could sit down, so he'd stopped going at all. And by the time the new stadium had been built he'd lost all interest anyway.

As Gethin chewed vacantly on a piece of toast, Gransha asked him what was up. Gethin's first reaction was to deny that anything was wrong. Then he sighed and told Gransha how he'd challenged Nathan – being careful not to mention too much about Caitlin and nothing at all about his time in the past with Guto. Gransha's eyes lit up as he listened –he was obviously over the moon to hear about Gethin's brave stand. But Gethin himself didn't feel brave at all by now. Yesterday's confidence had disappeared completely. What hope did he have of beating Nathan?

"*I'll help you, mun*," said Gransha, eagerly.

As his tad-cu began to talk about how he could help him train, Gethin only half listened. He never knew whether to believe what came out of Gransha's mouth, because Gransha had never been one to let the truth get in the way of a good story. He swore, for example, that even with a dodgy leg after a pit accident he could sprint faster than most men with two good legs, and that he'd hardly ever had to pay for his own pints because someone was always stupid enough to challenge him to a race between The White Lion and The Crown.

Gethin watched his tad-cu as he rambled on about his favourite runner, Emil Zátopek, and how the athletics world had been wowed by this strange little man; how Emil had trained in big, heavy shoes instead of normal running shoes; how he'd sprint around the track eighty – yes, *eighty*! – times, one circuit after the other, to build up his strength and stamina.

The more Gethin stared at his tad-cu, the more he looked like the Hen Ŵr y Coed – the Old Man of the Woods – until in the end it was impossible to tell which was which. And that's when Gethin realised that he should – for once – actually listen to Gransha.

"OK, that's great, Gransha," he said, when he could get a word in edgeways. "How about starting Monday? I don't have school because it's a teacher training day."

Gransha's eyes twinkled with happiness. Then the two of them agreed not to say anything to Gethin's mam, because she'd be sure to put the kybosh on the idea.

So this would be Gransha and Gethin's secret.

And that felt really good.

25

When Gransha told Gethin he'd arranged for an old friend to pick them up for their first training session, the last thing Gethin expected to see was a skip lorry pulling up outside the house. The battered lorry, like its owner, had seen better days. On the side of the cab were the words 'W.D. Jones Waste Management', although they'd faded so much it was hard to read them. Gethin's heart sank. If anything, Mr W.D. Jones looked even older than Gransha and almost as shaky. They hadn't even begun, but already today was shaping up to be a total waste of time.

Dressed in his running kit, Gethin followed as Gransha drove his mobility scooter down the ramp outside the house.

"*Billy, you old mucker. How's tricks?*" asked Gransha. "*This is the grandson, Gethin.*"

"*All right, butt?*" asked Billy, also in English, before helping Gransha to his feet and into the lorry's cabin then loading the scooter on the back.

"*Hop in, then,*" Billy told Gethin, climbing stiffly back into the driver's seat. Gethin joined Gransha. The lorry's cabin was just as scruffy as the rest, and it smelled damp and mouldy.

"*It's a bit shang-di-fang in 'ere, I know. But the old lovely still goes, that's the main thing,*" said Billy, starting her up and driving away.

Shang-di-fang! Guto and his mates were always saying that – it meant higgledy-piggledy, or topsy-turvy. But he'd never heard it before in the present day! Gethin's heart beat a little faster. Had Billy really just used an old Welsh saying?

Gransha noticed Gethin's surprise and grinned. "*Gethin speaks Welsh, mun,*" he told Billy.

"*Proper Welsh, most likely. Not like mine. Don't speak it much these days anyway,*" said Billy.

"Where do you come from?" Gethin asked him, in Welsh.

"*Top of the valley,*" answered Billy. In English.

"The Rhondda Fach or the Rhondda Fawr?" asked Gethin.

"T*old you 'e was a nosy little so-and-so,*" laughed Gransha, over the moon to see Gethin showing an interest.

"From the Rhondda Fach," answered Billy, in Welsh this time. And not just in Welsh, but with an accent just like Guto's! Billy saw the surprise on Gethin's face.

"*Told you I speak funny,*" he said, back to English again. He sounded a bit defensive.

"I don't think it's funny. I think it's great. I didn't know people still spoke like that, that's all," explained Gethin.

Billy's face softened. "*Last of the Mohicans, we are, see.* Only a handful of us left that talk like me. And every one of us as old as the mountains by now. Cymraeg y Gloran – Gloran Welsh, we call it. That's all Mam spoke, see. Her whole family

– as it happens – came from the same valley. Her mam's side, and her dad's."

Gethin was grinning from ear to ear by now. Hearing Billy's accent was like meeting an old friend.

"Where was it?" asked Gethin.

"Mam-gu's family was from Blaenllecha. And Tad-cu's from Llanwynno," explained Billy.

"My granny was from Llanwynno. On my mother's side. 'Mam-gu' she was to me as well, like. 'Ell of a character she was," said Gransha, suddenly.

"Llanwynno?" asked Gethin. He couldn't believe his ears.

"Aye. Lived in this little cottage up in the sticks all by herself. No toilet or running water in the 'ouse. Wouldn't speak nothing but Welsh to me. Smoked a pipe and all," said Gransha, smiling at the memory.

No wonder, then, that Gransha understood some Welsh, even though his mam hadn't spoken it to him. Gransha went on to talk about his tad-cu's family and how they'd moved here from County Durham in northern England, but Gethin wasn't taking much notice now.

All he could think about was that, maybe, Gransha's mamgu – Gethin's great grandmother – was the great, great, great, great granddaughter of someone he'd met three hundred years ago. Perhaps she was related to Guto, even! But before he could get too excited, Gransha added:

"Mam-gu's family weren't from round 'ere either, mind. They came down from the Beacons."

"Llanfrynach?" Gethin blurted out, on instinct.

"That's right. We went there once, lookin' for the old place.

Had a meal in the pub. I'm amazed you remember. Only a small little thing you were."

Gethin's head was spinning. So his roots really were in Llanfrynach. And then, more recently, in Llanwynno!

"How about we drive up to those tops today?" suggested Billy. "Great place to run, is Llanwynno."

"A *really* great place," agreed Gethin in a blink, slipping into the same accent without realising it.

Billy glanced at him in surprise before bursting into hearty laughter.

~

Gransha had warned him not to start too fast and Gethin didn't want to push himself too hard either, so he began by alternately jogging and walking, with Gransha driving beside him on his scooter. The lane that ran along the crest of the mountains was straight and pretty flat, after Billy had driven up the steep slopes and dropped them on the 'tops'.

It felt odd to be right back in the middle of the old parish. The place was so familiar, yet so strange at the same time. Yes, the little hamlet of Ynys-y-bŵl was quite a bit bigger now, and Gethin saw from the map that some places on the edge of the parish had grown from almost nothing – like Porth, the Graig Wen and Abercynon. But apart from that, Llanwynno was just as it had been in Guto's time – a scattering of houses amongst green fields and woods. Gethin half expected to feel the presence of his old friends, but apart from a sharp wind he couldn't feel anything up here. He began to jog faster, to try to keep warm.

Though Gransha had kept a sharp lookout all the way, they'd only passed one car so far. And apart from two women on mountain bikes who waved at them as they passed, they hadn't seen another living soul. Gethin was beginning to enjoy himself. He'd hit his stride now and he could feel the energy surging through his body as his blood pumped strongly and his legs moved in a smooth rhythm.

"*Let's get off the road,*" suggested Gransha, pointing towards a path that wound its way into a wood.

Gethin didn't recognise this wood, with its conifer trees standing straight and tall in rows on each side of the path. But as the path fell, he saw below him the remains of the old forests that had once covered the banks of the streams and rivers, and the slopes that were too steep to farm. He made out oaks, hazel and beech trees, to name just three, and he wondered at his new ability to name different trees. He'd not had a clue before. Guto had opened his eyes to the natural world. He felt a stab of loss, like a dagger in his side.

"*You look a bit iffy,*" said Gransha. "*Better stop a minute. Don't want to overdo it.*"

Then Gethin heard children, laughing together in the distance. He drew to a halt, straining his ears. Nothing now, but the whisper of the wind in leaves. Had he imagined it? No, he hadn't. Here it was again – laughter, dancing lightly on the wind. It was Guto and the gang, waiting for him. It had to be!

Gethin began to run again, heading towards the sound, even though his tad-cu was calling for him to stop. He was sprinting so fast now that Gransha had trouble keeping up with him, even on his scooter.

"Hold your 'orses, mun!" he shouted.

But the only thing Gethin could hear was his feet crunching on the path and the sound of the laughter as it grew louder and louder. The trees around him began to thin and an open glade appeared in front of him. He knew the place at once. Daerwynno Farm!

Gethin was pushing himself to his very limits. All he knew was that he was dying to see his old friends again, and that they'd be overjoyed to see him too. But even before he came bursting into the farmyard he realised something was wrong. Yes, there was the farm – no doubt about that. A neat, square little house with stone steps at the side of the building, leading up to the attic. But the doors and the windows had been painted green. And everything looked much too new.

Then he saw a gang of schoolkids in climbing gear struggling up a climbing wall. It was they who were laughing. There was no sign of Guto or the others. Of course there wasn't. How could Gethin have been so stupid? The past had gone, and the door of time had slammed shut.

The children were staring at him in surprise. Gethin stood there, out of breath, and felt the disappointment bite into him. He turned to run back, the world about him misty through the tears that welled in his eyes. He didn't notice the thick branch that hung across the path until he ran straight into it. Wincing in pain, he gulped lungfuls of cold air. Suddenly his chest grew tight. It felt as if someone had poured a bag full of sharp slivers of glass into his lungs. Gethin couldn't run a step further.

He fell to his knees – right in front of Gransha's scooter.

26

The doctor was really kind. Although Gethin's mam tried to explain everything to her without letting her son open his mouth, she insisted on asking Gethin himself about his symptoms. Gethin didn't mention the trip to Llanwynno with Gransha and Billy. Instead he said he'd collapsed after running to catch the bus.

Then the doctor told him to describe how the attack had felt, before giving him a thorough examination. She asked him to blow into a strange-looking gadget, a sort of cross between a plastic pipe and a measuring jug. Gethin breathed in deeply before blowing out. The doctor made notes before asking Gethin to blow into it again and to try his very hardest this time. Gethin breathed in deeply for the second time before blowing with all his might – so much so that he wheezed. The doctor made another note before telling Gethin that by now she was pretty certain what the problem was: he had asthma.

As soon as he heard this, his stomach sank. Asthma! That must have been what floored him on Hallowe'en, too.

He hardly heard the doctor as she went on to explain that he'd have two different pumps now, to treat the condition – a brown one to stop the asthma and a blue one to take when his chest felt tight. And, although she reassured him that there was no reason why he shouldn't take part in physical activities, as long as he used the two pumps conscientiously,

Gethin had already persuaded himself that he would never, ever be able to run again.

The dream was over. He could forget all about the race now.

~

Gethin stayed in his room the following morning – his mam had given him permission to stay off school to 'rest'. He didn't feel like doing anything. Though he'd started using the brown asthma pump, he couldn't feel much difference. His mam hadn't thought much of the doctor's advice and had warned Gethin not to do any exercise, just in case. Gethin felt like telling her not to worry – after all, he'd never run another step. The asthma had put paid to that.

While he was resting in bed, thinking how true his mam's oft-repeated lecture was about life not being fair, he heard Gransha calling him:

"*Come down 'ere a minute, there's a good boy!*"

Gethin sighed and went down to the kitchen, assuming Gransha needed a hand with something. But Gransha didn't need anything. He was grinning from ear to ear. He'd been all the way to the town library on his scooter where he'd found lots of interesting articles about asthma, and he'd asked the librarian to photocopy them for him.

Now Gransha wanted Gethin to read them all, because they proved that lots of successful athletes actually suffered from asthma too.

"*If they can do it, so can you,*" he insisted, handing the photocopies to Gethin and telling him to take them up to his room before his mam came back from the shops.

Gethin thanked Gransha for going to so much trouble to help him, but inside he knew it was no use. How could he ever run again, now that he knew he had asthma?

As he started for the stairs he heard the front door open. Without thinking, he sprinted up them before his mam could ask what he had in his hands.

"Be careful!" came his mam's voice from the hall. "You're not well, remember?"

But Gethin had already reached the top of the stairs. Slamming the door shut behind him he threw himself on to the bed then set about reading every single article – from the headline to the closing paragraph.

And it was well worth it. According to one article, although one in ten people have asthma in the UK, as many as one in every three of the world's professional cyclists, half of all cross-country skiers, and even high numbers of international-level swimmers suffered from asthma.

But when he came to the last article he sat up suddenly, as if someone had pinched him, hard. It was all about Paula Radcliffe, the famous runner from England who broke the world record at the London Marathon, despite the fact that she had asthma. Of course! Gethin had read about her somewhere before, about how she'd fainted during training when she was about the same age as Gethin was now, then discovered that she was asthmatic. If she could win the London Marathon – *and* break a world record – surely Gethin could compete in a little local race!

Then Gethin realised that his chest hadn't hurt all day, even after rushing up the stairs to his room. The brown asthma pump had to be working already.

Maybe the idea of taking part in the race wasn't such a stupid one after all . . .

~

Gethin didn't have a clue how many laps of the park there were to go – all he knew was his legs hurt like mad. The idea was to try and run the same circuit comfortably fast but without pushing himself to the extreme – over and over and over again, with Gransha timing each lap.

"*Keep it up! Only one to go!*" Gransha shouted as Gethin passed him for the thousandth time – or at least that's what it felt like. Though he was exhausted by now, Gethin tried to relax and let his legs do the work. After all, they were well used to the route by now.

Gethin had been training on the sly for a good few weeks now – with Gransha at his side, true to his word. Gethin had drawn up his own training schedule, but it was a real help to have Gransha there to time him and spur him on when he got tired – exactly as Gethin had encouraged and spurred on Guto. Though he was nothing like as fast and as fit as Guto, Gethin was pleased with how training was going. He had talent, that was for sure – and what's more, he was really enjoying it.

As he cornered the last bend a tall girl stepped out in front of him, forcing him to swerve to avoid her before sprinting on towards the finishing line.

"Gethin!" someone called from behind him.

He didn't want to slow down because he only had fifty

metres or so to go, but he couldn't ignore that voice. He stopped, turned and stared in surprise at Caitlin. He hadn't recognised her because she was wearing a white karate outfit.

Her hair was tied back tightly and for once her eyelashes weren't dark and thickened with mascara; her lips not coloured in with lipstick. Caitlin tugged awkwardly at her tunic to straighten it and avoided his eyes. For a moment, it wasn't the confident Caitlin before him but Catws, clumsy and shy. Then Gethin realised that he hadn't blushed. In fact, if anything, there was a hint of pink on Caitlin's cheeks.

"This outfit's even more shapeless than school uniform."

"How long have you been doing karate?" asked Gethin.

"Since I was little. No one at school knows. Not even Nathan. Maybe I'll tell him when I've got my black belt," she added.

"What colour are you now?" asked Gethin.

"Brown," answered Caitlin. "And before you ask, black's next."

Gethin laughed. Caitlin could deck almost any boy in class then. Just like Catws.

"You're surprised, aren't you?" asked Caitlin.

"Not really," said Gethin, without explaining why. Caitlin wouldn't believe him if he told her. No one would.

"I almost didn't recognise you, either," she said. "You run really well."

"Yeah, well, I've been training," said Gethin, not wanting to give too much away in case she reported back to Nathan.

"Don't tell anyone about the karate," blurted Caitlin, suddenly.

"I won't – if you keep quiet about my training," answered Gethin as he saw Gransha approaching on his scooter, coming to check he was OK. "Gotta go. See you," he said hurriedly, beginning to run again.

"I really liked the present. The one you made for me," called Caitlin, but Gethin was too far away by now to hear her.

Gransha was waiting for him, a grin on his face.

"*Who was that then?*" he asked.

"Just someone from school."

"*Nice looking girl,*" said Gransha, eyeing Gethin with a grin.

Before Gransha could ask any more nosy questions, Gethin suggested they start for home.

About halfway there it started raining, hard, and the two were sopping wet in no time. Gethin didn't care and neither did Gransha, though he could hardly see where he was going through the driving rain. He was entertaining passersby with loud snatches of songs about rain, like '*I'm singin' in the rain . . .*' and '*Raindrops keep falling on my head . . .*' Some looked suspiciously at him, others joined in.

When they reached home, they rushed about to get changed, get dry and hide their wet clothes, which Gransha planned to take to the laundrette tomorrow so Gethin's mam would be none the wiser. Then Gethin wiped the scooter dry, for the same reason.

When Mam came in the two of them were sitting comfortably on the sofa, watching TV. She stuck her head round the door.

"Have you two been sat in front of that set all day?" she asked.

"What else are we supposed to do? Look at the weather, Mam," answered Gethin.

"*Aye. It's tippin' it down, mun,*" agreed Gransha.

Tut-tutting, his mam closed the door. And the two of them began to laugh – quietly, so she wouldn't hear.

27

Gethin turned the key in the front door and pushed it open. His mam was working late tonight so Gethin and his tad-cu planned to go out running straight after school. Obviously, Gransha wouldn't be running – as ever he'd be following Gethin on his scooter, timing his progress.

"Gransha! I'm back!" he shouted.

"In the kitchen!" came the answer. But it wasn't Gransha. It was his mam.

Gethin went through to the kitchen.

"Where's Gransha?" he asked. Then he saw that his mam's eyes were red from crying.

"In hospital," she answered, drying her tears. "He's very ill."

Gethin wanted to put his arm around her, but he couldn't move. He was frozen in place.

His mam rose from her chair.

"I've got to go round now. Do you want to come with me or stay here?" she asked.

Gethin tried to speak, but no sound came from his mouth.

"I'm going upstairs to change. Make up your mind before

I come back down," she said, walking out of the kitchen.

Gethin wasn't sure if he could face going to the hospital, but maybe staying at home on his own would be even worse.

~

Because the plastic chair creaked loudly every time Gethin moved, he tried to sit as still as possible so as not to draw attention to himself.

He'd been waiting in the corridor outside Gransha's ward for ages, while his mam talked to a nurse at the reception desk. A bald old man hobbled past, leaning against a younger man with a shaved head, who had an arm around him. Gethin tried not to stare at them but there was something so uncanny about the way their heads shone in the bright lights of the corridor that he couldn't help it. The old man noticed and smiled at him, and Gethin looked away.

At long last, his mam came back. Though she tried to reassure Gethin that Gransha was in very good hands, her face was pale.

"What's wrong with him?" asked Gethin, nervously.

"Pneumonia," answered his mam. "Like flu but a lot worse."

Maybe Gransha got ill after that soaking we had on the way home from the park, Gethin thought. He felt his own lungs tighten and reached for his blue asthma pump. That was better. His lungs relaxed – but the guilt was still there.

"Is he . . . is he going to be OK?" asked Gethin. He was afraid to hear his mam's answer but, at the same time, he had to know.

"It's too soon to say," she said. "But the nurse sounded quite positive," she added. Gethin wasn't sure whether his mam was telling the truth or just trying to lift his spirits.

The ward was a long room with a row of beds up against both walls. As Gethin walked in he was careful not to stare too much at the other patients and to keep close to his mam. When he lifted his eyes he saw Gransha in the bed at the end of one of the rows. His eyes were closed and he was struggling to breathe. Sitting down at his side, his mam gestured to Gethin to do the same. Then she held Gransha's hand and kissed it, but it was as if he didn't even know they were there.

A malicious little voice whispered in Gethin's mind that Gransha would die, and it would all be Gethin's fault.

28

But Gethin had forgotten how tough Gransha was. He wasn't about to let an attack of pneumonia get the better of him. After ten days he was back home, in good time for Christmas. Gethin loved seeing his mam make such a fuss of Gransha, instead of lavishing all her attention on him. And, even better, it was obvious that Gransha didn't blame Gethin at all for what had happened.

On the first day of the holidays an unexpected visitor came to the house. Apart from the time he'd picked Gethin and Gransha up for training, Billy Skips hadn't called by like this before – at least not since Gethin and his mam had moved in with Gransha. Gethin was really pleased to see him and Billy was delighted to see Gethin too, greeting him with a mouthful of Cwm Rhondda Welsh. Helen stared at Billy in surprise – she'd never heard him speak Welsh before. But the thing that surprised her most of all was that Gethin and Billy obviously knew each other.

"We met that day we went up to Llanwynno," said Gethin, without thinking. He regretted it at once.

"When did you go to Llanwynno?" asked his mam.

Gethin's heart-rate was speeding up and his chest was tightening. He'd really put his foot in it now.

"Well?" she snapped, sensing something underhand. But Gethin's mind had gone blank and his tongue wasn't working. He could feel his heart pounding in his chest, which was starting to wheeze.

"We went on a little trip to show Gethin the area, seeing as his great grandmother lived there," Billy broke in.

"*That's right. And to show him where Guto Nyth Brân came from, like. You know – for his school project,*" added Gransha.

The old men's minds were sharper than Gethin's, who was still racking his brains for an explanation. Helen's eyes lit up.

"What a lovely idea."

"Bobby asked me. I couldn't refuse," said Billy, winking at his friend.

"*That was very thoughtful of you,*" Helen told Gransha in English before turning to Gethin. "Why didn't you tell me?"

"I forgot," answered Gethin, feebly.

"Tell me – what'll I do with you?" asked his mam, ruffling Gethin's hair affectionately before heading for the kitchen to make everyone a cup of tea.

"*That was a close one,*" said Gransha. And the two old men began giggling like naughty boys.

Gethin took a puff on his blue pump to quieten his chest and Gransha opened the box of chocolates Billy had brought as a gift and offered them round. Gethin chose a white one. It melted on his tongue and as he swallowed it the sweetness slipped down and seemed to soothe his chest almost as well as the pump.

"I brought a little something for you, an' all," said Billy, passing Gethin a package.

Thanking him, Gethin opened it. Inside its careful wrappings was an old book from the year 1888 called *Plwyf Llanwyno: Yr Hen Amser, Yr Hen Bobl a'r Hen Droeon* – or *The Parish of Llanwyno: Bygone Days, Bygone People and Bygone Stories.*

"It was Mam-gu's. She treasured it. Present from her tad, see," explained Billy. "I'm sure she'd like you to have it."

"I'll look after it really carefully," promised Gethin, fingering the dusty cover, deeply touched by such a thoughtful present.

~

Gethin closed the book and put it on the arm of the sofa. It was Christmas morning and he'd just finished reading it. The style of the book had been a bit flowery and longwinded, and the language was a little unfamiliar sometimes, but Gethin had devoured every word. In fact, his mam kept complaining that he'd done nothing lately but sit with his nose stuck in it. She was only pretending to be annoyed, because inside she was pleased to see him taking such an interest.

But reading the book had been a bitter-sweet experience for Gethin. On the one hand, it'd been great to learn more about the place he loved and be reminded of his time there, as lots of the same local customs and practices were still remembered and followed when the book had been written. Guto was still remembered too. But on the other hand, reliving everything had been painful, like opening an old wound.

His nostrils filled with the smell of Christmas dinner, drifting into the living room from the kitchen. Then he listened. An unfamiliar sound was drifting this way too. He smiled as he realised it was his mam, singing happily to herself. She'd decided to celebrate Christmas in style for once and worked extra hours so she could afford a big turkey and all the trimmings.

Because she'd been so busy preparing Christmas dinner, they were all going to open their presents after the meal. Gethin didn't mind at all. There was something nice about having to wait for them. What's more, last night when Gethin's mam had been doing a spot of last-minute shopping, Gransha had given him some secret presents – a pair of running shoes and a running vest, ordering Gethin to hide them before Helen got back.

"Dim ond un seren . . . un seren . . ." came his mam's voice, singing a Welsh Christmas tune and twirling into the living room. Gethin almost fell off the sofa. Not only was she singing but she was dancing, too! Then she grabbed him and pulled him to his feet, before whirling him around the room in a clumsy waltz.

"*Been at the sherry already, 'ave you?*" joked Gransha, sticking his head round the door.

"*I'll leave that to you,*" Helen retorted, letting go of Gethin. Gransha laughed, showing the gap in his teeth.

"*And put your teeth in while you're at it. Food's almost ready.*"

Gransha laughed again and rubbed his belly greedily as if he was starving.

He needed his teeth too. Gethin couldn't remember ever having such a Christmas feast. He ate a heaped plateful and then had second helpings too. Everything was so delicious!

"Leave a space for the pudding," warned his mam.

"I'll eat the pudding, don't worry. And the mince pies, later on."

"I've noticed you've been eating much better lately. I've no idea where you put it all – you're still as skinny as a rake."

Gethin knew very well why he wasn't putting on weight – his running burned up all the calories.

"*You couldn't 'alf put it away yourself, mind,*" Gransha told her through a mouthful of turkey. "*And I'm not just talkin' 'bout food either,*" he added, winking at Gethin.

"Dad!" Helen scolded, but her eyes sparkled with laughter.

"*Remember that Christmas you finished off your mother's Babycham? Livid, she was.*"

And then Gransha told them stories about all the scrapes

Helen had got into when she was a teenager. Some of them were pretty surprising, especially the one about her and her friend sneaking off to Cardiff to see a heavy metal band when they were fourteen. And they'd nearly got away with it – but, unfortunately for them, their picture had appeared in the *Western Mail* the very next day.

"Still, wouldn't 'ave changed you for the world," said Gransha, his eyes twinkling.

Gethin's mam took another swig of wine, trying to hide the little grin that was spreading across her face. She was actually blushing!

Then she stood up to fetch the pudding. That tasted wonderful too, and the white sauce was perfect. But even better than the sauce was Mam's wide smile, lighting up her whole face. And it was an infectious smile. Gethin's cheeks hurt as he beamed back. And Gransha too was grinning from ear to ear. Gethin looked from one to the other of them and felt himself fill with happiness. His mam had been transformed, Gransha was back from hospital and Gethin was ready for the race.

This is the best Christmas ever, he thought, happily. And they hadn't even opened their presents yet.

~

Two days later Gethin was kicking himself for daring to believe that everything was fine. It *hadn't* been the best Christmas ever. Not by a long shot.

It had all gone wrong so suddenly. The three of them

were in the living room, playing a new board game that Gethin had been given as a present. OK, there'd been plenty of leg-pulling and the odd shout of disappointment when the dice hadn't gone someone's way, but everyone had been enjoying themselves . . . until Gethin won and Gransha let the cat out of the bag.

"*Quite a champion we've got on our 'ands. You'll soon see now New Year's Eve.*"

Gethin's heart leapt to his throat. Gransha and his big mouth. The twmffat!

"What's happening New Year's Eve?" asked Helen.

"Nothing," said Gethin, looking at his feet.

"Gethin?"

"*Tell her, mun. Nothing to be ashamed of.*"

It was obvious that Gransha had had one sherry too many. Gethin had no choice but to tell his mam about the race, and about how he'd been training for it with Gransha. Helen listened without a word, but Gethin saw the worry, the disappointment and the anger in her eyes.

"You could've got ill again . . ." she said in the end.

"But I didn't, did I?" Gethin protested.

". . . never mind dragging Gransha out in all weathers."

"*Listen 'ere now. I'm old enough to look after myself, and so is the boy.*"

Helen ignored Gransha.

"How could you have gone behind my back like that?"

"What about all the times you went behind Gransha and Mam-gu's backs when you were young?" asked Gethin, feeling himself getting angry now that the shock of Gransha's revelation had passed.

"That was different," snapped his mam.

"How?"

"Because it was me, that's how. OK?"

"So. One rule for you and another for me, is it?"

"You're not running in that race, and that's the end of it!" thundered his mam.

"*That's your problem – always overreacting,*" put in Gransha, which really didn't help matters.

"*You keep out of this,*" snapped back Helen.

"*If you don't let the boy 'ave a crack I'll come back and haunt you when I'm gone. And that's a promise.*"

"*Don't be so stupid.*"

"Shut up!" shouted Gethin. "I've had enough – of both of you!"

Gransha shut up and Helen stared at him in surprise. Gethin had never raised his voice to them like this before.

"There's no such thing as ghosts. The past is the past," Gethin told his tad-cu, before turning to his mam. "I hate you. You always spoil everything!"

He knew he'd gone too far this time, but he didn't care. His mam had turned completely pale and looked as if she was about to cry.

"Go to your room. Now!"

"Don't worry – I'm going."

Gethin strode towards the door and slammed it shut behind him, so hard that the whole house shook.

29

There was no escape. Gethin battled his way up the slope through the thick, black forest. With every step he took the bloodthirsty beast closed in on him. And then all went silent. The same, unnatural silence as before. And the same darkness. The only sound was Gethin, breathing hard. In no time, the monster would leap on him. It would open wide its maw and foul, sour saliva would drip down to soak his face. Its claws would pierce his chest, penetrating his ribcage and tearing it apart.

This wasn't fair. He'd tried so very hard. And he'd overcome so many obstacles. Would this be his destiny for ever? Being ripped to pieces by this filthy beast – this creature that didn't even have the guts to show itself before attacking? In his rage, he turned to face the monster.

It was even more hideous than he'd imagined: long, mangy tail, powerful, hairy body, huge, orange head, like a rotten pumpkin. Carved into the pumpkin's rind was a familiar face. And, though its eyes were so very green and its vicious teeth so yellow, there was no doubting who the monster was. It was Gethin himself.

Gethin opened his mouth wide and let out a deafening scream. To his astonishment, the beast disappeared in a puff of smoke.

~

Gethin woke, dripping with sweat. Darkness. Silence. Only the sound of Gethin's lungs, wheezing. Where was he? Back in the woods of Craig-yr-hesg?

No. He was safe in his bed.

He battled to control his breathing then remembered the blue asthma pump. The relief came immediately. One puff and the pain disappeared – like the monster.

A shiver went down his spine as he recalled how abominable it had looked. And its face – his own face! Another shiver went through him, but not because of the monster. Something had just occurred to him. Something crucial.

It wasn't Nathan he had to beat, or his mam, or anyone else – the only person stopping him doing what he wanted was himself. And with that realisation, he made a decision.

He was going to run in that race, come hell or high water.

30

The train journey from Pontypridd to Mountain Ash, where the race took place, lasted just quarter of an hour, but to Gethin it felt like for ever.

He got off the train and felt the cold wind bite at his face. Gripping his blue asthma pump tightly – he'd need to take it before the race – he walked to the meeting place to collect his number. The street lights made everything look unreal.

The situation felt unreal too – Gethin still couldn't believe he'd disobeyed his mam. Gransha had been delighted, of course, when Gethin had told him what he'd decided. Together they'd come up with a plan to get Gethin's mam out the house. Gransha had asked her for a lift to Billy Skips's house, to wish him a happy new year – and by the time they got back it'd be too late to stop Gethin taking part.

He was at the meeting place now, telling the woman giving out the numbers his name. He half expected her to ask where his parents were, but all she did was wish him good luck. Gethin tried to smile at her but he was too nervous.

Pinning his number to his vest he went back to the street and checked his watch. Quarter past five. There was almost half an hour to go before his race – the third of the evening. Looking up he saw there was a square opposite the starting posts. In it was a statue. Gethin went to get a closer look and found himself standing, stock still, in front of it. He could hardly believe his eyes. It was Guto – or at least how the artist had imagined Guto – as a young man. His face wasn't totally right and the cheeky grin was missing, but there was something about the statue that really showed his speed and his stamina. Running at his side was a greyhound, and Gethin smiled as he remembered Guto racing the local sheepdogs.

"Ready?" asked a voice.

Gethin turned. It was Nathan – with Cai at his side.

"Yes," answered Gethin, as confidently as he could.

"We'll see, eh?" said Nathan, striding away with Cai tagging along behind him, as obedient as Mabli, Catws's goat.

"What on earth have I done, Guto?" Gethin whispered to the statue.

But there was no answer.

~

Gethin tried to stand as close to Nathan as he could at the starting line. This wasn't easy because so many runners were taking part – there had to be close to fifty. Lots of them looked really professional too, wearing proper, running-club shirts. He saw a blue Cardiff vest, a black Aberdare one, and Nathan was wearing one in black and white – Pontypridd colours – over his T-shirt. Thanks to Gransha's secret Christmas presents, Gethin didn't feel too out of place, though everyone else was almost a head and shoulders taller than him. Before, that would have worried him, but not any more.

The course was much shorter than the adults' one – only one circuit around the nearby streets – but Gethin was ready for it. He'd prepared so thoroughly that every turn in the track was seared into his mind. He looked about him at the crowd of spectators. Evan, Dawid and Jordan had told him they'd be here, but there was no sign of them anywhere. He felt a pang of disappointment, then he shook himself. There was no time for that – he had to concentrate.

Three. Two. One. Bang! Gethin hurled himself forwards. There was a sharp right-hand bend just after the starting line and Gethin was determined not to get stuck behind someone slow. Once he'd cornered the Workingmen's Club, he found himself sinking into his rhythm, feet hitting the ground lightly and smoothly. Then he caught a glimpse of Evan in the crowd, with Dawid and Jordan behind him – they'd come after all! Even better, Gethin was making good progress, beginning to catch up with Nathan . . . until he caught someone's foot and stumbled.

As he fell, he saw Cai, throwing him an evil grin as he ran past. Gethin hit the ground, hard, and pain shot through his ankle.

"Get up! You can still win!" shouted Dawid from the crowd.

"C'mon Gethin!" yelled someone else, even louder.

Caitlin.

The crowd roared their support as Gethin leapt to his feet and began running again. After a step or two, the pain in his ankle faded. At least I'll be able to finish the race, he thought, *but there's no hope of beating Nathan now.*

The next moment, a gust of wind gripped him by the scruff of his neck and dragged him forwards. It was just as if Guto was at his side, running with him, step by step. For the next few moments he was back in Llanwynno, running down the steep slopes of Cefn Gwyngul, so fast his legs felt like they were working separately from the rest of his body. Then he came out on to a flat section of the course, and realised that his legs were still moving just as swiftly and smoothly. In fact, if he hadn't been concentrating he'd have flown past the next turn and missed it completely.

Now he was sprinting down the final straight, the finishing line visible in the distance. A murmur went through the crowd as a slight-looking figure, smaller than the rest, wove its way through runners, easily overtaking them. A hundred metres to go. Fifty. Gethin had almost caught up with the fastest group of sprinters.

Nathan was leading them, with three girls behind him. But just before the finishing line the girls made the elemental mistake of slowing too soon. With only a metre or so to go, Gethin passed them. They hadn't seen him coming.

As he crossed the finishing line the crowd went crazy. What a race! And what an amazing performance from the runner who'd tripped at the start!

He'd been sprinting so hard for the line he had trouble stopping and he bowled straight into someone in the crowd.

"Sorry," he panted, trying to get his breath back. He lifted his head.

Looking down at him was his mam.

The two of them stood stock still, not saying a word. Gethin's heart was beating hard – and not just because of the race. Then his mam took a step towards him.

"Turned out Billy Skips wasn't home," she said, frowning. "I got the truth out of Gransha in the end. You shouldn't have gone off without telling me."

Gethin's heart sank. Then she went on, "But I'm very proud of you all the same."

The next moment, she was wrapping her arms around him and giving him a big cwtch, right in front of everyone. But Gethin was so glad she'd come to support him he didn't care who saw.

~

The crowd roared as Gethin mounted the podium to take his medal for second place. It was an even louder roar than Nathan got next, even though he'd won. Nathan reached down to shake his hand in congratulation and this got another roar of approval from the crowd – with no one shouting louder than his mam. The Tri Trist were clapping their hands and whistling, so proud to be Gethin's friends. There was no sign of Cai anywhere.

After the awards had been presented, everyone waited in excitement to see which famous person would come to light the torch in Guto's memory. It was a different person each year, and their identity was always kept a tight secret. But, as a tall, strong, upright man strode through the crowd carrying a flaming torch, Gethin recognised him at once – it was Wales's rugby captain! When he lit the torch next to Guto's statue, the flames danced around Guto's face and Gethin swore he saw the statue smile at him.

Then came the fireworks. To Gethin's surprise, his mam agreed to stay on to watch them and Evan, Dawid and Jordan joined them to see the sky explode in a fiesta of red, white and green.

Gethin saw Nathan and Caitlin walking past, hand in hand. His heart almost stopped when he saw who was with them. It was a middle-aged man – and he was the spitting image of Richard Edwards. The man turned, saw Gethin and headed straight for him.

"Excellent! Very well done!" said the man. His accent was a little jerky, as if he'd learned Welsh, rather than grown up speaking it.

"You're Nathan's dad," said Gethin. It wasn't a question – it was a statement.

"Ha, ha! Yes," laughed the man. "How did you know?"

"You look alike," said Gethin, though they didn't really. Gethin couldn't exactly tell him that he looked just like someone who'd lived three centuries ago.

"Bendigedig!" said Nathan's dad, which meant 'fantastic'. "*I love that word,*" he added, in English.

"Dad's learning Welsh," Nathan explained.

"*I'm from Southampton* – originally. Ha, ha!" said his dad, laughing again. He laughed after almost every sentence.

"Happy Now Year!" he went on.

"New," corrected Nathan.

"*Of course.* New. Ha ha ha!"

Then Nathan took to Gethin to one side. Gethin followed him, obediently. After all, he was Nathan's lapdog now, because he'd lost the race.

"Listen," said Nathan. "If Cai hadn't tripped you, you'd have won – so the bet doesn't count. But I'm going to leave you alone from now on, whatever. And from what I've seen, you're well able to handle Cai yourself."

"Thanks," said Gethin. He couldn't think of anything else to say.

"Don't thank me. Thank Caitlin. It was her idea."

As Nathan and his dad turned to go, Caitlin came over.

"I'd like us to be friends," she said, staring shyly at the ground, just like Catws.

"As long as you don't treat me like a cute little mascot – OK?"

"I won't, I promise. Friends?" she asked, putting out her hand.

"Friends," agreed Gethin, shaking it.

Then she turned and hurried back to Nathan and his dad, who was still laughing about something. Gethin saw the smile Nathan gave her, saw the reflection of the colours of the fireworks on her face as she smiled back at him. Nathan looked like a completely different person. Someone softer, kinder, less angry with the world.

Gethin didn't care that Caitlin and Nathan were happy together. Caitlin and he were friends – maybe even real friends, for the first time. And that was more than enough for him.

31

"Iechyd da!"

Gransha raised his pint glass in a toast and Gethin and his mam lifted their glasses of lemonade to clink them all together.

The three of them were sitting, warm and cosy, in the pub opposite Llanwynno Church. After the race, Gethin's mam had grounded him for a week for going behind her back. Then she'd asked him where he'd like to go as a treat, expecting him to say Cardiff or somewhere like that. She'd been surprised when he'd said this pub in the middle of nowhere, but she was more than happy to come when Gethin explained he wanted to visit the area where his hero, Guto Nyth Brân, had lived. Billy Skips had driven them here.

After they'd eaten a lovely roast dinner, Gransha started on one of his favourite stories. Although he'd heard it many times before, Gethin – and his mam – chuckled in all the right places and the afternoon flew by as they talked, laughed and just enjoyed each others' company. *This is how it should be*, thought Gethin, smiling. Something told him that this was the first of many happy afternoons for the three of them.

While his mam paid for the food, Gethin sneaked out of the pub. There was one more thing he wanted to do, on his own this time. He crossed the road, pushed open the iron gate and stepped into the churchyard. The finely-built stone church looked very different to the simple meeting-house Gethin had visited so often, three hundred years ago, but the hills around it were the same. Thanks to Guto, he knew all their names – Twyn Mawr, rising from the Cynon valley, and Cefn Gelligaer and Cefn Eglwysilan, which lay beyond the river Taf. In the other direction was Cefn Gwyngul – Guto and the gang's favourite haunt.

Gethin didn't have to look long to find the grave stone. He read the words out loud, just as they were carved, in Welsh, on the stone: "In memory of Griffith Morgan of Nyth Brân in this parish who died in the year 1737 at 37 years old. He was a proficient runner. He beat one of the name of Prince of Bedwas Parish in a race of 12 miles, which he completed in seven minutes less than an hour."

Gethin quickly did the sums in his head. Incredible! This more or less equalled the world-record speed for a half-marathon. If Guto had been alive today, he would have been world famous.

Then a gust of wind gripped the scruff of his neck, just as it had during the race.

"Are you there?" whispered Gethin.

In answer came the sound of cawing. A crow was sitting at the top of one of the graveyard's trees, staring straight down at him. But this wasn't an ordinary crow. It was a white one.

If ever you see a white crow, run for your life! Gethin shivered as he remembered Guto's mam's words. But he stood his ground and, when he looked up again, he saw that there was something dearly familiar about the bird. Something he couldn't explain.

Gethin held his breath as the crow flapped towards him and landed on a nearby grave. It croaked in greeting, playfully tipping its head to one side. Then it beat its wings and, in a wink, it was perching on Gethin's shoulder and cawing again, non-stop – the nearest thing to laughing Gethin had ever heard a bird make. In fact, he could've sworn that the crow was smiling at him. A very familiar smile.

"Guto?" whispered Gethin, so as not to frighten it.

"Ge-thin! Where a-are you?"

His mam was calling him, without any of the usual impatience.

"Co-ming!" Gethin called back.

With one last croak, the bird beat its wings and rose into the air. It flew higher and higher and higher, a little white spot in the sky that grew smaller and smaller. And then it disappeared altogether.

Gethin wasn't sure whether he'd ever see the white crow again, but he was sure of one thing: venturing through the door of time had changed his life completely. He smiled as he threw a last glance at the grave stone before hurrying out of the churchyard to his mam and Gransha, into a new world – a world full of possibilities.

Afterword: The Historical Aspect

Very little is known about the life of Gruffudd Morgan, or Guto Nyth Brân, and most of the little we know comes from a book by Glanffrwd (William Thomas) about the history of the parish of Llanwynno, which was first published in 1888. (This is the book, in the novel, that Billy Skips gives to Gethin at Christmas). We learn that the year of Guto's birth was 1700. At the time, his parents lived on a small farm called Llwyncelyn, above the Rhondda River, before they moved to the permanent family home a stone's throw to the east, Nyth Brân. Guto became a famous athlete and won several races, before dying as a young man aged 37, in front of his girlfriend Siân, after a tough twelve-mile race against an opponent called Prince.

Those are the bare facts. But many stories grew about him. It was rumoured that he was fast enough to catch a hare or a bird, or even get to bed before the room darkened after he had extinguished his candle. It's also said that once, his mother, who was preparing tea, asked him to fetch sugar from the store in Aberdare and he returned before the water had boiled on the fire!

I read Glanffrwd's book in detail as part of my research before starting on the novel. It's an interesting book for several reasons. In terms of Guto's history, it's striking that the author remembers hearing these stories about Guto as a child from people who in turn heard them from people old enough to have known Guto himself. Similarly, many of the old customs and ways of doing things – the world as Guto would have known it – were still alive when Glanffrwd wrote his book, despite the fact that the Rhondda area had changed enormously due to industrialisation. Today, on the other hand, most of the features of Guto's time have disappeared.

Things change, yes, but not everything changes all at once, or even at the same pace. Some aspects of life can remain similar for many years, if not centuries. Others change within a generation, or even sooner. If you think of technology or social media, for example, then it's almost impossible to keep up with all the changes! It may be very hard to imagine a life without Instagram or TikTok today, but some other innovations will surely take their place at some point. (When I wrote the novel, which appeared in 2017, Snapchat that was all the rage).

Let me give you another example. I remember, as a child, being amazed at the fact that my father lived through a time when there was no electricity at his family home – and no toilet or water supply either – water had to be carried daily from a nearby water source. Candles and paraffin lamps lit the house, which was heated by an open fire. To put this into some kind of perspective, my father would have been the same age as Gethin and Guto in the novel during the last year of the Second World War, 1945.

My father's home was a smallholding, a house with some land attached to it. His parents kept a cow, some pigs, a handful of chickens, and grew vegetables in the garden. The cow would give milk, and my grandmother would make butter from it. One of the pigs would be killed every year and the meat cured. The chickens would supply eggs. As well as cultivating his land, my grandfather worked for the farmers of the area when the need arose. And during the important seasonal periods, everyone would come together to do the work together, sharing resources.

This was basically no different to how Guto would have lived over two hundred years earlier – and, indeed, generations before that too. For many, many centuries therefore, rural life remained largely unchanged. If my father, as a child, had landed in Llanwynno in 1713 and spent a year with Guto, he would have coped much better than I would have. And if Guto had landed in the north of Ceredigion – or any other Welsh speaking agricultural area, for that matter – before the end of the Second World War, it would have been far less of a shock to him than landing in contemporary Wales.

Yet, this is only half the story. Despite so many similarities, Guto would have been amazed at many aspects of life, even then. Although horses were still in use, it wasn't a horse that transported my grandfather from place to place, but a motorcycle. If you wanted to go somewhere far, like London, for example, you didn't have to follow the old drovers' route and walk for many days but rather you could take a train from the local station and arrive within a few hours. (In fact, the train network in Wales was far better then than today!) Unlike earlier generations of my family, all of whom came from Ceredigion and only moved a few miles after getting married or to find work, two of my grandfather's brothers worked in the south Wales coal mines. And it was here they stayed for rest of their lives. My grandmother, for instance, was born in Pontypridd before returning to her parents' birthplace as a young girl to live with her aunt and uncle. Although she lived her life in her new home entirely through the Welsh language, she wrote to her siblings, who still lived in south Wales, in English. Their world had expanded, and new technology, the radio, was bringing the world into the home.

The engine which drove this change was the industrial revolution that had begun a century and a half earlier – a revolution that was to completely transform areas such as the Rhondda and, later, rural enclaves like Llanwynno. At the same time, there was another revolution in the way people chose to worship. Starting as a trickle in Guto's time, a vast wave of people eventually left the established church for the various nonconformist chapels. Arguably, these two very different, but interconnected, revolutions were most influential in shaping modern Wales and, just as importantly, the way the Welsh came to see themselves. Of course, Wales has changed a lot in recent decades in very many ways, but these remain two very significant foundation stones amongst the many on which contemporary Wales was built.

So, there were two main challenges when writing the historical part of this novel. The first was that, unlike Glanffrwd in 1888, I had no direct link to the early 1700s. In order to get an idea of Guto's time I therefore had to turn to books of all kinds, and searched in libraries, archives and online for other resources e.g. various records and maps of the period to try to create as vivid a picture as possible. The National Museum of History at St Fagans is also a great place to live the past, incidentally. The second challenge was the period itself, which was on the eve of the industrial revolution, i.e. before all the changes that helped to shape the Wales we know. Because Guto's Wales wasn't just some old-fashioned version of Wales today, but, in very fundamental ways, a different Wales altogether.

To give just a few examples: this was a Wales where almost everyone spoke Welsh, and only Welsh. A Wales much smaller in population – for every ten people today there would only be one then – and the vast majority of those three hundred thousand depended, in one way or another, on the land. The seasons, and the weather, would rule everything. If the weather was bad, as it was during 1700-1710, there would be a shortage of food. There were no such thing as supermarkets or even shops as we know them today, so people would go hungry and sometimes die of starvation.

This was a Wales without a capital city – Cardiff was a small, relatively insignificant town. (And the biggest town? Have a guess! The answer is at the end). A Wales where the roads were so terrible it was easier to move goods around the coast by shipping. A Wales where, for the most part, people stayed in their own area. And those people, in an attempt to make sense of the world around them, believed not only in the ancient saints and the power of holy places, such as St Mary's Well in Penrhys, but also in magic, and the 'Tylwyth Teg', the little folk ...

What, then, of Llanwynno, Guto's home, in the early 1700s? As mentioned in the novel, Llanwynno is in Glamorgan, and Glamorgan was divided – in landscape and culture – into two main parts, the 'Blaenau' in the north and the 'Bro', the 'Vale', in the south. Broadly speaking, the Vale was more fertile and wealthier than the uplands of the 'Blaenau'. Because of the relatively poor quality of the land, in the uplands keeping animals was more important than growing crops. According to records, each farm had about 20-30 cows, 50 sheep, six goats, and also a few pigs and chickens. Smaller farms, and smallholdings, kept a horse, about 30 sheep, about four cows and their calves, two or three pigs, and a few goats and chickens. The farm instruments and utensils were simple and made of wood, and people would share them. People would also come together to carry out important tasks, such as shearing, straw cutting and harvesting. Unlike in the Vale, wheat was not the main crop but rather barley and oats, which provided a more aromatic and darker bread, and porridge. And apart from festive days, here's what would be on the menu: barley and oat bread, 'llymru' (a kind of porridge), and a thin soup with the occasional bit of bacon. However, the butter and cheese were of high quality, and Caerphilly cheese is famous to this day.

Perhaps one of things you found most surprising in the novel was that all the residents of Llanwynno spoke Welsh – not only that, but they couldn't speak English either. This was true of the whole of upland Glamorgan and, as I've already mentioned, 90% of Wales at that time. The situation was more complicated in the Vale. In some areas, English was the main language. This was because parts of the Vale, along with Gower and southern Pembrokeshire, were once 'Englishries', i.e. areas settled by Norman, English and Flemish people in the Middle Ages. Other parts of the Vale, such as the town of Cardiff, were bilingual. But Welsh was the predominant language of the surrounding villages and beyond, such as Radyr, Lisvane and Whitchurch – now all part of the City of Cardiff.

In the original version of the novel, it becomes immediately obvious that the type of Welsh Guto spoke was very different from 'standard' Welsh today. Jane, the translator, has done a great job of alluding to this by making Guto's English slightly strange. The Welsh spoken in south-east Wales at the time was a dialect called 'Gwenhwyseg' – 'Gwentian' in English – which was still very widely spoken up until the second half of the twentieth century.

Perhaps the most exciting find during my research was a tithe map of the area from the eighteenth century held at the Glamorgan Record Office. This map was so detailed not only did it outline the different fields belonging to Guto's home, Nyth Brân, but also their names. It was just like having an ancient version of Google Maps – amazing! Field names are usually very old and very descriptive, so it was possible to imagine how these different fields might have looked and how they were used.

I also had photocopies of two old maps on the wall at my computer while writing the novel. One was of the parish of Llanwynno, the other of east Glamorgan. The names of the farms, rivers and hills were therefore at my fingertips, and if the wind roared outside and drowned out the noise of the city, I would sometimes imagine I was on the slopes of Cefngwyngul, or Craig yr Hesg, and not in front of my laptop.

Oh, yes. Before I forget – the answer to the puzzle. The largest town in Wales in 1713? Carmarthen!

About the Author

Gareth Evans started his career in radio, before turning to scriptwriting. He spent a decade abroad, first in Spain, then Germany, before setting up home in Cardiff. For the past twenty years and more, he has been part of the writing team for the BBC's longest running TV drama series, the Welsh-language production, 'Pobol y Cwm'. He is currently working on a trilogy for young adults, set in 6th century Britonia, northern Spain. The first part of the trilogy, 'The Magic Hornpipe', has also been translated into English.

Acknowledgements

Thanks to Richard and Iwan for introducing me to the language of Glamorgan in the 18th century, to Rhian for answering my questions about the Rhondda area today, to Gordon for his wise advice, to Anwen for her care, to Anne for the cover, to Myrddin for his patience, and to Anna for her invaluable suggestions and happy collaboration.

A big thank you also to Jane, who translated the novel, for her meticulous, inclusive approach, for the many enjoyable Zoom sessions, and for the polished end result.

About the Translator

Jane Burnard is a highly experienced editor, who, having learned Welsh, has recently added translating to her bow. Her translations include the aforementioned 'The Magic Hornpipe' and 'Paint!' Originally from Cumbria, Jane is also a novelist in her own right. Her first novel, 'The Thirty Third Owl', was published in 2021 and her second, 'The Cry of the Red Kite', appears Autumn 2022.

Novels steeped in history

Exciting and subtle stories based on key historical events

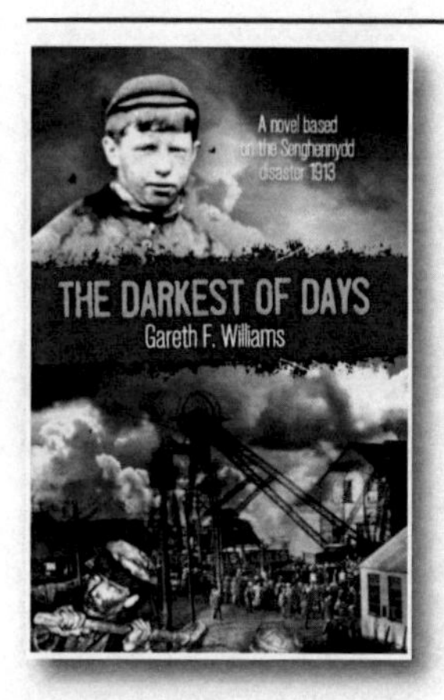

THE DARKEST OF DAYS
Gareth F. Williams

A novel based on the Senghennydd disaster 1913.

£5.99

Winner of the 2014 Tir na-nOg award in the original Welsh

THE MAGIC HORNPIPE
Gareth Evans

A gripping story set in Britain, 552 AD, following 12-year old Ina's perilous journey escaping from her enemies. Her only company is Bleiddyn, her wolfdog, and in her bag, the magic hornpipe.

£8.50

WESTERN WILDFIRE
Ifor Wyn Williams

Gruffudd ap Cynan, the fighting flame against the Normans

The story of Gruffudd ap Cynan's fight to regain his kingdom in Gwynedd.

£7.95

THE EMPTY ROOM

Angharad Tomos

A Welsh family's fight for a basic human right 1952-1960.

Shortlisted for the 2015 Tir na-nOg award in the original Welsh

£5.99

PAINT!

Angharad Tomos

Why are they painting roadsigns in Wales? Why are they painting the town?

It's the summer of 1969, and a turbulent time in the history of Wales.

Shortlisted for the 2016 Tir na-nOg award in the original Welsh

£8.50

WOVEN

Angharad Tomos

A shocking story of a slave girl in the West Indies and a servant maid in Wales, and the terrible suffering that accompanied slavery.

A historical novel that faces facts and greed and violence ...

Shortlisted for the 2021 Tir na-nOg award and Book of the Year in the original Welsh

£8.50

THE IRON DAM
Myrddin ap Dafydd

A novel full of excitement and bravery about ordinary people battling to save their valley from being flooded.

£5.99

Shortlisted for the 2017 Tir na-nOg award in the original Welsh

THE MOON IS RED
Myrddin ap Dafydd

A fire at an RAF bombing school in Llŷn in 1936 and bombs raining down on the city of Gernika in the Basque Country during the Spanish Civil War – here's the story of one family at the centre of both events.

Winner of the 2018 Tir na-nOg award in the original Welsh

£6.99

UNDER THE WELSH NOT
Myrddin ap Dafydd

"you'll get a beating for speaking Welsh ..."

Bob starts at Ysgol y Llan at the end of the summer, but he's worried. He doesn't have a word of English. The 'Welsh Not' punishment for speaking Welsh is still used at that school.

£7.50

THE CROWN IN THE QUARRY
Myrddin ap Dafydd

The world's largest diamond ... in Blaenau Ffestiniog.

The story of evacuees and moving London's treasures to the safety of the quarries during the Second World War.

£7

THE BLACK PIT OF TONYPANDY
Myrddin ap Dafydd

It is 1910, a turbulent time of disputes, strikes and riots in Cwm Rhondda, when the miners are fighting for fair wages and better working conditions.

People from different backgrounds are thrown together, resulting in friendships and conflict ...

£7.99

FASTER THAN THE SWORDS
Myrddin ap Dafydd

It's Summer 1843 – the time of the Rebecca Riots. The teenage twins of Tafarn y Wawr in Llangadog find themselves caught up in the struggle and they need to learn from the gypsy Mari Lee how to run faster than the swords ...

£8.50

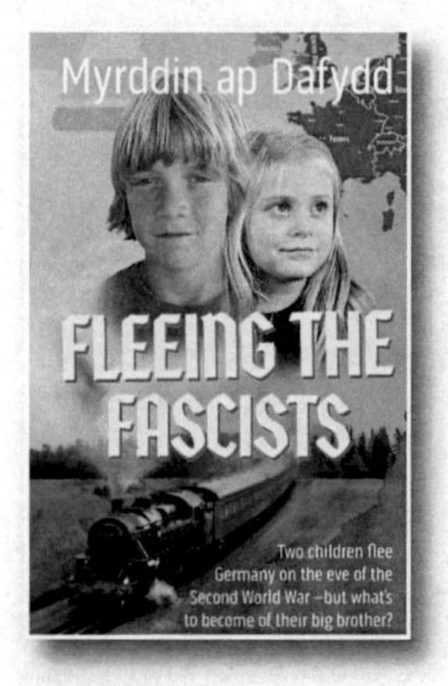

FLEEING THE FASCISTS
Myrddin ap Dafydd

Two children flee Germany on the eve of the Second World War.

Their family find refuge in Aberystwyth in Wales, where a pre-war friendship at the Urdd's Llangrannog camp gives hope for the future.

£8.50

BLACK RIVER
Louise Walsh
(*suitable for Young Adults*)

Harry Roberts is a Cardiff journalist haunted by his failure to cover the Aberfan disaster. *Black River* is a powerful piece of investigative drama that draws on the feelings of a wounded nation to show the good and bad aspects of journalists, politicians and villagers alike.

£7.50

RUNNING OUT OF TIME
Gareth Evans

Life is not easy for 13 year-old Gethin. Following a Halloween party he wakes up in the year 1713 and meets one of his heroes, the legendary runner Guto Nyth Brân.

£7.95